GUM DROP DEAD

EMILY JAMES

STRONGHOLD BOOKS

Cover Design: Mariah Sinclair at www.mariahsinclair.com

Published December 2020 by Stronghold Books

Print Book ISBN: 978-1-988480-28-2

Ebook ISBN: 978-1-988480-27-5

ALSO BY EMILY JAMES

Maple Syrup Mysteries

Sapped: A Maple Syrup Mysteries Prequel

A Sticky Inheritance

Bushwhacked

Almost Sleighed

Murder on Tap

Deadly Arms

Capital Obsession

Tapped Out

Bucket List

End of the Line

Slay Bells Ringing

(also contains a Cupcake Truck Mystery novella)

Rooted in Murder

Guilty or Knot

Stumped

Cupcake Truck Mysteries

Sugar and Vice

FREE TIPS FOR AMAZING CUPCAKES

Each book in the Cupcake Truck Mysteries includes a cupcake recipe, but even when you have a great recipe, baking the perfect cupcake can sometimes be hard.

To receive the top 10 tips for amazing cupcakes (inspired by the Cupcake Truck Mysteries sleuth, Isabel), sign up for my newsletter at www.subscribepage.com/cupcakes.

(If you're already a member of my newsletter, no need to worry. I've emailed you a link to the tips too!)

1

*W*orking in the food truck I'd leased after mine was burned to the ground still felt like wearing someone else's underwear. Until the insurance company sorted everything out, though, leasing was all I could afford.

My business partner Claire turned around, her arms full of a tray of cheddar, basil, and peach muffins. I grabbed the tray right before it smashed into my midsection. Having a second person in the truck with me was going to take some getting used to.

And as if working in a strange truck and working together for the first time wasn't enough, we'd decided to make our debut of savory "cupcakes" at the hot air balloon festival.

Claire let out a huff. "This will be easier once we have a routine. It'll just take us some time."

She said it like I'd already suggested dissolving our trial partnership. It'd take something more than a few stepped on toes and ribs in elbows for me to give up on the idea.

I could get more catering jobs with savory options in my repertoire...and Claire needed the money. She still hadn't found a full-time job after months of trying, and even with me renting her spare room, she wouldn't be able to keep her house. Not unless she either got a job or her skeezie, cheating husband decided to divorce her and pay her alimony rather than continuing to live with his new girlfriend. Nope, I wasn't going to leave a friend to struggle, even if helping wasn't feeling convenient all the time.

"It'll help if we can eventually get a bigger truck too," I said.

Leasing had required me to downsize to a smaller truck. The insurance company claimed it wouldn't be much longer before they'd pay out my policy. Apparently, they'd never dealt with a case before where the vandal had also been a murderer who'd stolen a vehicle and set it on fire to frame someone else. My insurance agent claimed that was creating some unique challenges since the criminal case was ongoing.

I couldn't see how. My truck was stolen and destroyed. The details shouldn't have mattered. It probably served me right for going with the cheapest policy I could find. At the time, I hadn't been able to afford anything better.

Claire made an affirmative noise, but her attention was already on making sure the chalkboards where we displayed our menu and prices were set at the perfect angle. A few months ago, her apparent fussiness might have driven me batty. Now I saw it for what it was. Claire dealt with nerves by controlling everything she could.

"Excuse me," a man's nasally voice said. "I have a question about one of your products."

I set aside the bowl of buttercream I'd been scooping into a piping bag and stepped closer to the counter.

I almost stepped backward again. His skin was both pasty and puffy, and his nose and the skin surrounding it were red. The hand he'd rested on the counter clutched a tissue that I could only pray was clean. He looked like he ought to be home in bed rather than walking around a hot air balloon festival, sharing his germs with everyone he came close to. Especially given he looked to be in his sixties.

I forced my lips into a pleasant, welcoming smile. "Which product?"

The man sniffled. "Your tropical cupcake. I want to make sure it doesn't have any lime juice or zest in it." He waved his hand frantically around his head. "And you really should do something about all these flies."

I barely stopped myself from glancing at Claire. Unless I needed glasses, there weren't any flies. The day wasn't even warm enough for them yet, the morning unseasonably cool for August. Maybe he was high or drunk rather than sick.

But I couldn't assume that was also why he asked about lime. He might have an allergy.

"The tropical cupcakes are mango curd and coconut. No lime or citrus of any kind."

He puckered his face up as if he were holding back a sneeze. It went on so long that I shifted my weight, and Claire glanced in my direction.

Finally, he breathed out. "I'll take one of those."

Not what I would have expected for six o'clock in the morning, but to each his own. I'd eaten cupcakes for every meal of the day and almost every time in between, so I really wasn't one who could judge. Our tropical cupcakes didn't even look healthy, though. They were covered in toasted coconut and orange and yellow gum drops.

He paid, and I handed him the cupcake, making sure not to brush his fingers. Whatever he had, I didn't want to catch it. He swatted at the flies that only he could see and took a bite. Then he turned his back to us, but he didn't move away, as if he were waiting for someone.

A shorter man, wearing jeans and a red t-shirt that read Cloud Chaser Balloons, huffed toward us. He carried a hat in his hand.

"There you are," Sniffle Man said. "I've been waiting for fifteen minutes."

The shorter man crushed his hat. "I'm trying to do you a favor."

His voice was soft, but his hat didn't look like it would survive the encounter. I felt a little like the emotional version of a Peeping Tom. But it wasn't like Claire and I could move our truck away. Unless the men left, we were basically trapped spectators.

I glanced at Claire to see if I could mime *should I clear my throat and remind them we're here?* Claire studiously wiped down the counter, even though she'd wiped it down before our odd first customer showed up. She didn't look up. Apparently her tactic for the situation was denial.

I couldn't do that. I'd spent too much time being hypervigilant to be able to pretend that whatever was happening between the two men wasn't happening.

Sniffle Man swiped his tissue across the bottom of his nose. "It doesn't feel like much of a favor. I don't know why I even agreed to come."

"Because—" The shorter man's head snapped toward our truck as if he'd realized he had an audience.

I averted my gaze on instinct, even though it was like broadcasting the fact that I had been eavesdropping.

"I need to get up in the air for the opening ceremonies," the shorter man said. "Come with me. It'll be the most private place to talk."

I peeked up under my eyelashes. The shorter man reached for Sniffle Man's arm. Sniffle Man jerked away. But he followed him.

I wouldn't have gotten into a hot air balloon with someone I clearly didn't like or trust. But that wasn't saying much. I wouldn't allow myself to be placed in any situation where I didn't feel safe and have an escape route.

Claire moved beside me once they were out of earshot. "It's a good thing I'm too practical to believe in omens."

Even if the weird start to the day turned out to be a harbinger for the rest of the weekend, it still had to turn out better than the last festival I'd attended.

"At least the ground here is too hard for someone to dig up a body," I said.

Claire harrumphed. "Let's not tempt it."

2

*T*he timer on my cell phone went off with the ten-minute warning. The officials at the festival were supposed to drop the green flag at 6:30 am to signal the all-clear for the opening day mass ascension. Claire had asked me to set a timer for her. She was supposed to meet Dan and Janie, so they could watch together while I manned the truck.

The grounds had already filled up with spectators despite the early hour. According to the spiel from the organizer who'd called to say I'd gotten one of the waitlist spots, the weeklong festival drew tens of thousands of spectators. Only a fraction of those people would be interested in cupcakes, and most not until after the mass ascension, so Claire and I had decided that we'd take turns exploring the festival each morning. With Dan and Janie coming today, I'd suggested she should go first.

She made change for our single customer and handed her a

cheddar and bacon muffin. Claire was still holding out against my suggestion that we call them mock-cakes, but a cupcake food truck selling muffins somehow felt wrong.

"I changed my mind." She slid the money into our money box. "You go."

That hardly seemed fair. Dan was her cousin, and she was "Auntie" Claire to Janie. She should be the one who joined them. I'd have a chance another day.

Claire held up a hand before I could open my mouth to argue. "Don't. I hate hot air balloons anyway. Dan and Janie don't need me ruining their excitement. Dan'll be as much a little kid about all of this as Janie."

I could see that. Despite what he must have experienced as an undercover cop, and then having his brother and sister-in-law die suddenly, he managed to grab at joy in a way that I didn't quite understand. But I liked to watch. Maybe someday I'd figure out the secret too.

Still. It felt like Claire was only saying all of that to make me feel better. "No one hates hot air balloons."

Claire's eyebrows went up as if to say *are you calling me a liar?* "Mike proposed to me in a hot air balloon, even though he knew I was afraid of heights. I know now that he probably did it because he wanted to go for a ride and wanted a way to justify the expense. I was incidental." She pressed her lips into a line. "That probably should have been a clue about the selfish jerk he'd turn out to be, but things are always clearer looking back."

I'd learned that the hard way as well. Looking back, I could see all the warning signs that my husband wasn't a good man either. At the time, I'd been able to explain everything away or ignore it.

Claire pointed toward the front gate where Dan and Janie would already be waiting. "You'd better hurry. You don't want them to be paying so much attention watching for one of us that they miss the liftoff."

I almost threw Claire a salute but thought better of it. We'd be working in tight quarters for the next week. No need to get on her bad side.

I hurried past the row of vendors between me and the spot Dan had arranged to meet Claire, but I made a mental note to take a little more time on the return trip. There was a vendor selling small stained-glass works of art depicting hot air balloons. Now that I was sleeping in a bedroom rather than a truck, I had a stationary window. I could buy something like that and put it up. Something to commemorate my step toward freedom.

The closer I got to the ropes dividing the spectators from the hot air balloons, the warmer the air became. Voices carried on the air as the operators called instructions to their crews. The air right below the balloons already shimmered from the flames filling them with hot air.

"Isabel!"

I turned. Dan waved to me from a bit further down. He'd laid a big blanket out on the ground. Janie sat beside him.

Sat might have been generous. Drooped against his shoulder might have been more accurate. They'd have had to be up before six o'clock to make it here, park, and find a spot to sit. Claire and I had been up since four, packing everything into the truck and then setting up once we arrived. It'd been a huge advantage to be roommates as well as business partners.

I sat next to Janie, and she immediately squirmed over to snuggle in against me instead.

"I wondered if Claire would back out given her history."

He was too much younger than Claire to be able to remember when she got engaged, but he'd no doubt heard the story many times since then. The smile Dan sent my way along with his words made me think he didn't mind the switch.

I nodded but didn't have a chance to say anything more. A weird hush fell over the crowd like everyone knew the mass ascension was only seconds away.

Before I could even finish the thought, the signal went out, and the balloons began to move. I nudged Janie, and she roused enough to sit up.

The balloons taking off was like watching a rainbow form. They were in the brightest colors and patterns imaginable. Today all of them were traditionally shaped, but on Tuesday, there'd be a competition for the most original specialty balloon. The website had shown balloons from past years in the shape of bees, and frogs, and even a dinosaur. Dan was hoping to bring Janie back that day, but his job meant that he could never be certain about his days off. If he caught a murder investigation, he might have to work. A few of Dan's other cousins were planning on bringing their families that day, but I knew Dan hoped to be able to see Janie's face himself.

Janie had pulled away from me and was pointing out her favorite balloons, all signs of sleep gone.

I shared a smile with Dan over her head. There was something about experiencing events through a child's wonder that made them sharp and fresh.

A yell drifted down from one of the balloons. I looked up, but I couldn't pinpoint which balloon it came from. It couldn't be one that was too high yet or I doubted we'd have been able to hear anything.

The basket of one of the lower balloons rocked. I strained my ears. If I concentrated, I could hear men arguing.

Janie didn't seem to notice. Her head swiveled from side to side, clearly trying to take in everything at once. Dan, though, followed my gaze.

Someone dangled out over the edge of the basket, and I sucked in a breath. My heart pumped so hard in my chest I thought it might burst.

"Stop!" The voice from overhead was clearer this time—a man's—though I couldn't tell whether it was coming from the person hanging out of the basket or someone still inside. "What are you doing?"

And then he was falling.

And screaming.

People around me gasped in what felt like a chain reaction, and a few screamed as well. Members of the ground crews scrambled out of the way.

I grabbed Janie and pressed her face into my chest. She squirmed.

"I need you to sit still for a minute, sweetie," I whispered urgently into her hair. I couldn't let her see this. No one should see this. "For me. Please. I'll tell you when you can look again okay."

She wriggled again. "Why?"

"It's a grown-up thing."

But not even grown-ups should have to see it. The Positivity Project column I liked to read in Lakeshore's newspaper once featured a story about a man whose parachute didn't open properly while he was skydiving, but he miraculously survived. Maybe that would happen here. The balloons were much lower than a skydiver.

Janie stilled. Dan clamped his hands over her ears. I looked away, but with my arms around Janie, I couldn't cover my own ears.

I knew the moment the man hit the ground.

3

*E*verything that happened in the next few minutes blurred together. Dan launched over the rope and ran toward the body, people all around me were dialing 911, telling the story on repeat, and Janie was asking me what was happening. I hurried her back to Claire, who stood out front of our truck, her hands pressed to her mouth.

My stomach felt like it fell down a flight of stairs. I'd been hoping Claire had at least been spared, but the dazed expression on her face said she'd seen the man fall, even from this distance. She'd probably been able to hear the screaming too.

Why was it that every event I attended ended up with a dead body? First the birthday party for Claire and Dan's grandfather, then the sandcastle competition, and now this. At least this time my contact with whoever had died was limited to being at the same event.

Claire lowered her hands, fisting them against her legs. "I told you those things were death traps."

"What's a death trap?" Janie asked.

I shifted my gaze toward Janie pointedly, hoping Claire would catch my *not in front of the kid* meaning.

"A death trap is a vehicle that's risky to ride in," Claire said. "Like a car that's so old it doesn't have seat belts."

Janie wrinkled her forehead. "Is there one of those here?"

Claire could find her own way out of this one.

I slid Janie's hand into Claire's and headed back toward the scene of the crime…accident? Right now, it could be either, though based on the yelling before the fall, an accident seemed highly unlikely.

Going back was probably unnecessary. There wasn't going to be anything I could do, but I'd learned my lesson about leaving. If a dead body turned up in your vicinity, it was better to stay put, whether you had anything useful to contribute or not. Leaving made police suspect you.

Even though it seemed unlikely that they could find a way to suspect me for this death, I wasn't taking a chance. Hopefully they didn't want to take a statement from me. I hadn't seen anything that everyone else wouldn't have seen, including Dan. And they could give their real names. I couldn't.

Dan had spread the blanket we'd been sitting on a few minutes ago out over the man's body. What had been a living person was now nothing more than a lump. A shiver trembled down my spine. Life was so fragile. And it was so easy to take for granted that you'd get a tomorrow when you might not.

A balloon touched down out in the middle of the field, and sirens wailed into the clearing. Two police cruisers. More sirens approached. Probably the ambulance, not that they needed to hurry at this point.

Dan flagged down the officers and showed them his badge, then headed toward where I stood by the edge of the rope. Many members of the crowd had already sneaked away, so I'd probably chosen to stay when I could have gone. It figured I'd make the wrong choice.

Dan stayed on the opposite side of the rope, indicating that he planned to help with controlling the scene at least until the detective who'd be taking over the case showed up. The female officer who'd arrived in the second cruiser moved toward the crowd, a notebook out, probably to take statements. A male officer joined her.

Dan's hands wrapped around the rope next to where mine sat, as if he wanted to take my hand but wasn't sure how I'd react. I wasn't sure how I'd react either. Part of me wanted nothing more than for someone to hug me. I felt numb in a way that the survivor part of my brain told me could be shock. Another part of me knew that, if he touched me at all, I might start to shake and not be able to get myself back under control. I couldn't have that happen.

Dan edged a hand closer. "Did Janie see anything?"

I shook my head. "She has no idea what's going on. I told her there was a problem with one of the balloons, so they'd be closing the festival. Claire though..."

Dan nodded as if that was all the explanation needed.

"Is he dead?" a man's voice yelled. The voice sounded vaguely familiar.

Dan turned around, and I moved to the side so I could see as well.

The short man I'd met before, wearing the Cloud Chaser Balloons t-shirt, huffed his way toward the younger officer standing next to the covered body. He'd lost his hat somewhere along the way.

My throat felt tight and dry. If he was coming to find out about the dead man, then it was likely the body under the sheet belonged to the sickly man who'd bought a cupcake from us an hour ago. They'd been heading up in a balloon together.

My mind spun with the idea that I'd seen the man alive less than an hour ago. He'd been walking and talking and eating. It didn't seem real.

The officer blocked the balloon operator's path before he could reach the body. "Are you the operator of the balloon the victim fell from?"

The man stumbled to a stop. "I knew he couldn't survive the fall. I knew it. But there was no way I could land fast enough to stop him."

The situation hadn't looked to me like the balloon was trying to descend at all until after the dead man fell from it.

But, then again, the angle we were at meant I might have missed it. Or maybe balloons lowered so slowly that I wasn't watching long enough. Once the dead man started to fall, I looked away. The operator might have been trying to bring the balloon down while the dead man was on board, but it didn't start working until after I'd stopped watching.

The female officer who'd been writing down witness statements moved over to the officer standing next to the body. She turned her back to the hot air balloon operator and leaned close to her colleague. I could see her mouth moving, but I couldn't make out what she was saying. The male officer nodded once, and she moved away back toward the crowd.

"I'll need to take your statement, sir." The young officer held out an arm like he was directing traffic. "Why don't we talk in the back of the car?"

The balloon operator stepped backward. "Am I under arrest?" He held his hands up in front of him in a back-off gesture. "I didn't push him. He fell out. I swear it."

I exchanged a glance with Dan, and Dan headed toward the situation. While he might not be on duty, he was clearly the person with the most seniority. He'd also likely dealt with the most murder suspects.

The balloon operator had jumped awfully fast to insisting that he hadn't pushed the dead man. The words I'd heard right before the man fell could have been spoken by either man. They could have belonged to the dead man, begging the balloon operator not to kill him. Or they could have belonged to the balloon operator, horrified by what the other man was doing.

But what reason could there possibly be for the dead man to have jumped from the balloon? If he'd wanted to commit suicide, there were easier, less painful, and much less public ways to go. Given that the men didn't seem to like each other much, this was probably going to be treated as a murder. Murder made the most sense of the evidence.

Dan had reached where the officer and the balloon operator faced off.

"I'm Detective Holmes." Dan held out his hand. The balloon operator shook it tentatively. "Officer Mandela is just trying to protect the integrity of the scene and make sure that whatever you say is private. Why don't you come with me instead? We don't have to sit in the cruiser if you'd rather not."

The balloon operator's shoulders edged down some from their position approaching his ears. "I don't understand what happened. We were talking, and then he was screaming about vultures trying to peck out his eyes, flailing around. I tried to tell him to stop before he upset the basket and killed us both. But then he..."

He made a motion with his hands, going up, then down, presumably miming the dead man falling out.

Dan was nodding along in a way that looked absolutely

genuine. If I hadn't known that Dan worked for years under-cover, I would have believed every second of it.

"Vultures?" the younger officer asked. "You're saying he jumped out of the balloon trying to escape imaginary vultures?"

The hot air balloon operator bobbed his head. "I know it sounds crazy, but that's what happened."

I'd heard the words shouted right before the men fell, but I hadn't heard anything other than incoherent yelling before that. While it was possible that the original yelling had been about imaginary vultures, it sounded pretty far-fetched.

The story was so preposterous that I couldn't blame the young officer for questioning it. Dan didn't give anything away by his body language about whether he was annoyed by the younger officer's reaction or not. No doubt he didn't believe the story either. Nor would whatever detective officially caught the case or the district attorney. The balloon operator was likely going to end up arrested for murder, and it'd be up to a jury to decide whether the cause of death was hallucinated vultures or being pushed.

Dan led the balloon operator toward the car.

"I didn't push him," the man was still insisting. "I didn't. I know how it sounds, but do you think I'd make up something so stupid if I did want to kill him."

The more he argued, the more guilty it made him seem. He probably didn't even realize it.

A text pinged in on my phone. It was from Dan.

Can you and Claire take Janie home with you? We need to hold him until the DA decides whether we already have enough to press charges. I can't leave the suspect unattended.

So Dan did believe this was a murder. At the very least, he believed there was a strong possibility. Otherwise, he wouldn't be worried about the balloon operator disappearing once he gave his statement.

How could an event that was supposed to be innocent and fun have ended with a murder?

Another text popped up from Dan. *I'm sorry. I know you didn't sign up to babysit today.*

Dan always acted like asking me to watch Janie was an imposition. I paused with my finger over my phone screen and glanced at the body covered by our blanket. The obvious reminder of how short life was.

I'd never told Dan before that having Janie around brought me more joy than a perfect batch of cupcakes. I couldn't even explain why I hadn't. Maybe it was because Jarrod seemed to take pleasure in taking away anything that brought me joy.

But as Dan had proven time and time again, he wasn't Jarrod.

And if I didn't tell him now, who knew if I'd have another chance.

I love watching Janie, I wrote back. *I want as much time with her as you'll let me have.*

Across the field, Dan glanced at his phone and then looked in my direction. I couldn't read his expression from his distance.

My stomach tightened. Great. That was probably a huge mistake. Now Dan would think I was some sort of clingy, needy interloper. Janie wasn't my daughter. This wasn't my family. Dan was my friend—the best one I had—but that didn't mean there weren't still lines I shouldn't cross.

I headed back toward my truck, sidestepping a funnel cake and coffee someone had dropped on the ground in the commotion. It was still so early in the morning that neither flies nor bees had come out to enjoy the feast.

A picture flashed into my mind of the dead man swiping at flies that weren't there when he ordered a cupcake from my truck. Vultures were a lot different from flies, but also not so different if neither of them existed.

The flies that only the dead man could see might be the only piece of evidence that could corroborate the balloon operator's story.

I glanced at where Dan was speaking to the balloon operator, to the lone male officer standing vigil beside the body, to the female officer working her way through the witnesses that had stuck around.

Don't get involved, Fear hissed in my mind. *Claire can tell them if anyone asks.*

In a way, I could see Fear's point. Making an official statement meant I'd be in the records. I'd be forced to either make a statement under a false name—which was a crime—or give my real name and risk Jarrod finding me. I didn't need to add fuel to that bonfire. After my friend Eve had set up a website for me as a surprise, complete with a picture of me, Jarrod could already be on his way here.

The problem was no one would think to ask about hallucinated flies. They wouldn't even think to interview Claire and I about the dead man. The only one who'd seen him come to our truck was the hot air balloon operator, and he wasn't likely to think what the dead man had for breakfast was important.

If the hot air balloon operator was innocent, I couldn't let him face arrest and possible prison time if I knew a detail that could spare him. But I needed to protect myself too.

I could think of only one way around it. I took out my phone and opened my text thread with Dan. My embarrassing words about how much I wanted to spend time with Janie stared back at me.

Heat burned along my cheekbones. I'd just pretend like I hadn't said it. I'd take whatever time Dan gave me, and I wouldn't be needy for more.

I typed in my message. *Before anyone presents the case to the DA, ask Claire about the man who bought a cupcake from us this morning and his obsession with flies.*

I slid my phone back in my pocket. With so many other witnesses, the police didn't need me. I'd done what I could for this case.

Now it was time to get out of here and hope that, in the chaos of this case, Dan would forget about what I'd said.

4

---

*J*anie and I were on the floor building a tower of blocks the next morning when Dan came in. He'd gone to the station straight from the hot air balloon festival to pull an extra shift. The press was already throwing ideas and rumors everywhere, and his captain had wanted to get out ahead of it if he could. Claire and I had kept Janie at our house overnight.

Thinking of it as "our house" still felt strange. And not as uncomfortable as I'd expected it would. Yes, someone could follow me home. That said, my name wasn't in any system. Claire and I had worked out the room renting privately. If she hadn't needed the money, I'd gotten the impression that she wouldn't even accept rent from me.

Dan swung Janie around and set her back on her feet. "Help

Isabel clean up the toys, and then go give Auntie Claire a kiss goodbye and grab your stuff."

Janie pouted out her lips, but she grabbed a handful of blocks and dumped them into the bucket. "Auntie Claire isn't here. She's at the gym again."

Again was a good way of putting it. After the hot air balloon festival shut down yesterday, I'd dropped Claire and Janie off and went to see if I could sell some of what we'd baked for the day. When I got back, Claire headed off to the gym. Barely twelve hours had passed between when she went yesterday and when she set off this morning.

I widened my eyes at Dan and tilted my head toward Janie. "Claire said she'd done too much taste-testing and needed to burn off the calories."

My big eyes and head tilt weren't the most subtle, but I wanted to let Dan know that I suspected there was more too it. Claire worked out regularly. Her gym membership was the one "luxury" she'd kept even when she tightened her budget. Without some sign, Dan might not realize I had a concern I wanted to mention when Janie wasn't around.

Dan helped Janie collect up the rest of the blocks. "Grab your stuff, and make sure to check everywhere, okay?"

Janie grabbed the bucket of blocks. "I'll put these away too."

Dan touched a hand to the top of her head. "Good idea."

We watched her go until she disappeared from sight.

"Is Claire not at the gym?" Dan asked.

"She's at the gym, but I think she'd there because she's struggling with what happened yesterday. She was up most of the night cleaning."

I didn't mention that the noise she'd made had kept me up most of the night too. I couldn't shut off my hypervigilance enough to ignore it or to use something to plug my ears. Janie, thankfully, had slept soundly through it.

Maybe I should have had trouble sleeping for other reasons. Maybe I should have been more upset, like Claire. I'd just seen so much death in the past two years. It wasn't that it didn't matter to me anymore. It wasn't that those lives didn't matter. It wasn't even that I still felt numb.

It was more that my mind seemed to adapt faster because of the practice. Life had to keep going. I had to keep going. Because I couldn't change the past.

My friend Nicole would have been so proud of me for figuring that out. I'd once wondered how she could handle facing so much death and evil in her job as a criminal defense attorney, or how her husband could manage it as the county medical examiner, or how Dan could handle it as a police detective. I think I'd finally figured it out.

They handled it because they believed that they could make the future better than the past as long as they didn't give up and let the past cripple them. Their hearts weren't hardened by what they'd seen. They just felt that giving up wouldn't fix what had happened. Working to prevent future similar tragedies would.

In this case, I wasn't actively investigating the potential murder, but I still had things I needed to do. I needed to watch out for Claire. And I needed to support Dan by taking care of Janie.

Thankfully, he hadn't mentioned my text. As long as he pretended like I hadn't sent it, we could also pretend that I hadn't overstepped my bounds and gone from *family friend* to *weird lady who seemed to want to play Janie's mom*.

"Do you know how much Claire saw?" Dan asked.

I shook my head. "She didn't want to talk about it, and we had Janie around until her bedtime."

I should make sure the house was as neat as Claire had left it at least. That way it'd be one less thing to make her feel stressed. I grabbed the throw blanket Janie had been using as a cape earlier and folded it.

Dan rubbed a hand along the back of his neck. The fine lines around his eyes were more pronounced this morning than they had been yesterday morning, probably because he couldn't have gotten more than a few hours' sleep last night. "I'll check in with her. It might help her to know that it wasn't a murder."

The words sent a jolt through my body, leaving my muscles feeling softer in its wake. I hadn't realized how much tension I'd been holding until that moment. The hot air balloon operator had been arguing his innocence fiercely. It was nice to know he'd been telling the truth. Maybe the text I'd sent Dan about the flies had helped. I hadn't heard if he'd talked to Claire about them, but I'd been away most of the day.

"How did you decide it was an accident?"

Dan collected up the remains of the snack Janie and I had earlier and headed for the kitchen. "The medical examiner found lime juice in his stomach along with a cough suppressant known as dextromethorphan."

My shoulders tightened again. They'd found lime juice in his stomach? That couldn't be right.

"The combination of the two can cause a lot of negative interactions," Dan was still talking. "Sleepiness and hallucinations are the most common. When those results came back, along with what Claire told me when I called about imaginary flies, it corroborated the hot air balloon operator's story."

That explained why he'd been seeing flies and vultures that weren't there. It even explained why he'd accidentally fallen out of the balloon. What it didn't explain was how he got the lime juice in the first place.

He'd asked about lime in my tropical cupcakes. That meant he must have known that whatever medication he was on could negatively interact with lime. He wouldn't have knowingly eaten any. Since he'd been careful about asking, it didn't seem likely he'd eaten any by accident either.

"The hot air balloon operator might not have pushed him out," I said, "but his death wasn't an accident."

5

I jerked awake. The room around me was dark, with only the moon shining through the window for light.

I sat up and stayed perfectly still. Dan had installed an alarm system shortly after I moved in. If someone had broken into the house, the alarm would be going off.

But something had woken me. The way my skin felt tight told me it wasn't simply my paranoia.

A buzzing whine made its way through the noise of the blood pounding in my ears. Was that…a vacuum?

I checked the clock. It was after one in the morning. And Claire had vacuumed less than two days ago. With the Northern custom of not wearing shoes in the house, the carpet couldn't have gotten dirty in that length of time. This was getting out of hand.

I laid back down and pulled my pillow over my head. The sound permeated through as a low drone.

The noise wasn't even consistent. It reminded me of snoring, where the sound rose and fell and changed, making it impossible for my brain to adapt.

Dan had said he would speak to Claire. He'd have done it by now. Dan never put anything off, especially when it came to the welfare of his family. So whatever he'd said to her hadn't helped or hadn't been enough.

I threw off my pillow and rolled over. Claire and I weren't exactly close. We'd established a professional rapport that allowed us to work well together, but we didn't even eat dinner together most nights. We weren't watching shows on TV together in the evenings or discussing our days. The most we talked was at Sunday night dinners with Dan and Janie.

But our time working together meant she'd spent a lot of time with me recently. Maybe she wouldn't shut me down immediately if I tried to talk to her. For both our sakes, the all-night cleaning marathons needed to stop.

I padded out of bed and down the stairs. Claire pushed the vacuum across the living room floor, changing directions to mark out perfect squares in the carpet. She'd pulled her hair back with one of the sweat bands she wore to the gym. Her face was grim and focused, as if she were performing surgery rather than cleaning an already clean floor.

"Claire?" I said.

She turned the vacuum again to reinforce the squares as if she hadn't heard me.

"Claire!" I yelled.

She jumped and turned the vacuum off. She turned around. "Oh. Did I wake you?"

I squashed the sarcasm that bubbled up inside. Sarcasm didn't come naturally to me. I really must be exhausted.

Claire hit the button to suck the cord back into the vacuum. "I don't know how Dan does it."

Her back was to me, but she had to be talking to me. She spoke loudly enough that I didn't think she was talking to herself.

She turned around and faced me. "How does he stop thinking about everything he sees? Every time I try to sleep, I see that man falling and hear the screaming. How do I move past something like that?"

I couldn't answer her question. I'd never asked Dan how he managed. Whether he dealt with it through prayer, a first responder support group, or private counseling, I got the impression that he liked to keep that part of his professional life separate from his personal life. And maybe that was how he managed, by keeping firm lines and leaving work behind as soon as he came home to Janie.

Claire didn't have that option of keeping work and personal life divided to deal with what she'd experienced. She was more like me—a normal person trying to deal with unexpected trauma.

"I don't know if you ever get over something like what happened." I sat on the couch, hoping she'd abandon the vacuum and join me. She stayed where she was. "I still sometimes see Jimmy, a homeless man I was friends with, when I close my eyes at night."

Since Claire already knew I'd been living in my truck, I told her all about how I'd met Jimmy. I'd shared with him what little I had in terms of food, and he'd shared with me much-needed friendship at a time when I felt more alone than I ever had. He'd been murdered shortly after we met, and I was one of the people who found his body.

Claire finally took a seat on the couch as well. "How did you manage to keep going after that?"

With Jimmy, I'd ended up helping investigate his death, somewhat unwillingly but it'd helped. Maybe that was my secret. "I tried to make it right."

Claire leaned forward as if she were at a lecture and wished she could take notes. "By investigating? Like you did when Grandpa died?"

When Claire and Dan's grandfather died, I'd investigated more as a means to protect myself. The police believed I'd played a role in it. At the time, Claire and even Dan believed I might have had some part in his death.

But that had been a trauma in itself—the uncertainty and fear. Investigating had helped me then, regardless of why I'd started to do it.

I nodded.

Claire stood up sharply and straightened her shirt. "Alright then. That's what we need to do. What's our first step?"

My brain felt like it was cartwheeling down a cliff, and I was scrambling to catch up with it. Claire had gone from distraught and nearly manic to businesslike faster than I could blink.

"Our first step in what?"

Claire huffed. "Investigating this man's death. Dan told me the police thought it was a murder, then an accident, and now it's officially been declared a murder again. We need to do something to help the police find the killer."

I'd seen Claire the Planner in action a couple of times. She'd orchestrated a huge one hundredth birthday party for her grandfather. She'd also helped me plan events on short notice. Having something happen that she couldn't control or change must have thrown her on a deeper level than either Dan or I realized. Latching onto the first proactive solution that presented itself made sense as a coping mechanism.

That didn't mean we should do it. "I don't think Dan will want us investigating. He's always been against me poking around in murder cases."

Claire planted her hands on her hips. "Did I say we were going to tell him?"

6

I clicked the seatbelt into place and settled the tray of cupcakes I'd baked to bring to the funeral luncheon on my lap. "For the record, I want to say that I think this is a bad idea."

"What record?" Claire glanced over her shoulder and pulled out of the driveway. She'd dressed entirely in dark gray and black, as if she'd been a close friend or family member of Donald Wells, the man who'd died. "No one's keeping a record. We're not even telling Dan unless we find something useful."

"It's a figure of speech. I meant that we didn't know the dead man, so we shouldn't show up at his funeral."

Claire glanced in my direction and raised her eyebrows. "You showed up at my grandfather's funeral, and you didn't know him."

Fair point. I'd gone to Harold Cartwright's funeral because I thought that one of his grandchildren might have killed him for the inheritance money. I'd been wrong, obviously, but I couldn't exactly argue that this was different. We were attending Donald Wells' funeral because it seemed like the best place to start looking for suspects in his murder.

Finding out his name hadn't even been that difficult. All I'd had to do was search for *murder at Lakeshore's hot air balloon festival*, and multiple articles had shown up.

The articles didn't name the operator of the hot air balloon, but they did say he was still a suspect. That told us that the police knew something we didn't, maybe a motive. We might be doing all of this running around for nothing.

I sneaked a glance at Claire. Not entirely for nothing. If it made Claire feel better and allowed us both to sleep at night, it'd be worth it.

Claire poked a finger at my cupcake tray without taking her gaze off the road. "What are those for?"

"We're going to the luncheon, so I baked cupcakes."

Claire cast me a sidelong glance. "It's not like a party. You don't bring a gift for the hostess."

My throat tightened slightly. As hard as I tried to be like everyone else and fit in, I kept showing how much I didn't know. I'd spent too many years first as a caretaker for my sick dad and then isolated as Jarrod's wife and then finally on the run and living in my food truck. I was in my thirties, but it often felt like

I knew less about life than a twenty-year-old just starting their adult life.

I hugged the cupcake tray closer to my stomach. "I've only ever been to three funerals. Two were my parents. The other one was your grandpa, and I didn't go to his luncheon."

Claire sucked her lips back in slightly as if, for once, she didn't know what to say. At last, she settled on, "Well. That explains it then."

Explained it but also left me with a tray of cupcakes in my lap. Why couldn't she have noticed what I was doing earlier this morning and asked me about it? "Should I leave them in the car?"

"Of course not. The buttercream will melt in the heat, and they'd go to waste."

I swallowed down a laugh. I was pretty sure Claire hadn't meant for that to be funny. It did make me feel better, though. Despite my mistake with the cupcakes, her reaction reminded me we had a surprising amount in common. In this case, our frugality.

Maybe it meant that we could eventually be friends the way Dan wanted us to be.

The way I wanted us to be. Living in a house with a person I wasn't sure liked me...well, it sometimes left me feeling like a house guest who'd overstayed her welcome.

I brought the cupcakes into the service with me and stored them under my seat. The funeral home where it took place was huge, and the room was packed with people.

Donald Wells hadn't had any children, but he did have a handful of nieces and nephews, all of whom sat in the front row along with his widow.

I mistook his widow for another niece until they played a slideshow, and it included wedding pictures. She wore a hat with one of those tiny veils that I thought people only wore in movies. It hid part of her face. Maybe she was older than the pictures made her look, but I would have guessed they had close to ten years between them at least.

The only other useful piece of information the funeral gave us was that Wells ran a financial services company that catered to wealthy clients. And that the luncheon was being held at the family home.

I checked the funeral program again as we filed out to be certain. I'd read it right. Donald Wells had been cremated. There wouldn't be an internment. Instead, mourners should come to the family home to pay their final respects.

As soon as we exited the funeral home, I pulled Claire by the arm out of the flow of people heading to their cars. "We can't do this. It's at their home."

Claire pushed the car's clicker, and a beep-beep answered. "That's an even better place to see what we can find out."

Her face wore the you're-not-going-to-argue-with-me expression that worked so well on Janie.

I deflated. I wasn't going to win this argument any more than I'd won any other disagreement with Claire in the time I'd known her. But if she decided to poke around in their medicine cabinets, I'd go wait in the car.

We drove through the business sector of Lakeshore, where the multi-story buildings blocked off the postcard-worthy scenery that the city was known for. I'd chosen to come to Lakeshore after Fair Haven because of how much larger it was. It wasn't until I arrived that I found out the city still managed to have a small town feel despite its size. The one part that felt like any other city was the downtown.

Claire's GPS sent us well past the business sector. The closer we got to the lake front, the bigger the homes got. The one with all the cars out front had to be at least three or four times the size of Claire's house.

I glanced at the back seat. Maybe I should leave the cupcakes behind after all. This went beyond not bringing a hostess gift to a funeral. These people were probably so fancy they didn't eat cupcakes. Not unless they were deconstructed and covered in goji berry powder or something.

"Don't even think about leaving those behind," Claire said. "They might help us start conversations."

And then she was out of the car.

We trailed behind a man and woman and followed them in through the door. There wasn't a pile of shoes at the door, so we kept ours on. Either they weren't originally from Michigan or the rules were different for rich people who probably had someone else around to clean their house.

Claire moved into the crowded part of the room. As far as I could see, there wasn't a buffet set out. I needed to find somewhere to put the cupcakes before I did anything else, otherwise the guests might think I was a server.

I wandered down a mostly empty hall that was twice as wide as an average hallway and came to a swinging door. A swinging door was the type of thing I could see being on a kitchen in a fancy house.

I pushed the door.

"It isn't right," a woman's voice said. Her tone was low, with a hiss to it, almost like she wished she could physically spit at him. "I was his *wife.*"

I froze with the door half open. I did not want to walk in on Donald Wells' widow. Not in the middle of her grief. Not in the middle of a private conversation. And certainly not without a better explanation for how I knew her dead husband than *I sold him a cupcake once, right before he died.*

"I know you're upset, Rebecca, but Uncle Donald left you a generous gift in his will. It's not the family's job to make sure you'll never have to work again. People who are capable of working should work."

Unlike her tone, the man's was calm and straightforward. His voice didn't carry any malice. He could have been reading from an accounting statement or a weather report for the emotion in his words.

At least we could cross Rebecca Wells off our list of suspects.

Assuming she knew about the contents of her husband's will, she wouldn't have had a reason to kill him. From the sound of it, she'd be worse off as his widow than as his wife. Whatever *gift* Donald had left her wasn't enough to let her live in luxury for the remainder of her days.

"This should still be my home." Rebecca's tone had taken on a whine to it now. "Donald would have wanted it to be my home. If you ask the rest of the family for leniency, they'll listen to you."

"If that's what he wanted, he wouldn't have had you sign a prenuptial agreement that said our ancestral family home would return to a blood relative when he died."

Without seeing the man's face, I couldn't tell if the hint of something I heard under his words was sarcasm or humor.

Rebecca Wells might not be a suspect, but whoever she was talking to could be. He sounded like he hadn't cared for Rebecca living off of his uncle's money. If whoever she was talking to felt the money she was frittering away should have belonged to him or a member of his family, that might have been a motive for murder.

Rebecca said something in a lowered tone. It sounded whiny, but I couldn't catch the words.

I leaned forward slightly. The swinging door swung the rest of the way in.

Rebecca Wells and the man with her both turned toward the door. The man had light brown hair that was curly enough that he clearly used gel to control it. He looked a few years older than me, and a few years younger than Rebecca.

He smiled at me. It actually looked genuine. "Were you looking for the bathroom?"

Something in the way he held his mouth told me that he suspected I'd been eavesdropping on their conversation. He didn't seem upset or annoyed by it. More amused.

Still, the last thing I needed was to draw the attention of someone who might be a murderer.

I extended my cupcake tray slightly. "I made cupcakes to express my condolences to Mrs. Wells."

Rebecca gave me a look that said she wasn't going to eat anything some stranger brought into her home, let alone a cupcake.

The man with her motioned me forward. I eased the tray down onto the kitchen counter and slid it gingerly in his direction. The door stayed wedged open behind me, letting the noise from the other mourners carry down the hall.

It also gave a direct view into the great room. Hopefully Claire was being subtle about her investigating. Otherwise, she'd give us away.

The man popped the top off the tray and glanced up at me. "These look amazing." He bit into one of the lemon meringue pie cupcakes. "They taste even better. Thank you for such a thoughtful gesture."

His voice softened at the end, and he glanced at Rebecca as if he expected her to agree. She mumbled something that I didn't catch again.

Silence fell, and I backed up a step. Time for me to leave before this got anymore awkward than it already was.

The man put the cover back on my tray. "Did you bake these or buy them? If they're from a bakery I don't know about, I'd like to be able to purchase more."

He's digging, Fear slammed into my brain with enough force that it almost took my breath away. *He wants to be able to find you later and get rid of you.*

Or, I argued back with my rational side, my cupcakes made an impression, and he really does want to know if he'll be able to get them somewhere.

So I could either tell him my name and potentially get more business or protect myself from someone who might be a threat.

The *might be* felt like an extra twenty pounds strapped to my back. The longer I went around carrying it, the heavier it would feel. Dan would tell me to take a chance on something good...or, at least, he'd tell me that if we weren't hiding this whole situation from him.

Dan would say that life wasn't worth living if I spent it being afraid.

I took out a card from my purse and handed it to the man. "They're from my food truck, How Sweet It Is."

Rebecca leaped up from her chair and swept down on me. Fear and all my instincts told me to shrink away or cower, say something—anything—to calm her down. But how could I do that when I didn't know what had set her off?

She brushed past me without giving me a sideways glance.

Relief flittered through my chest but didn't land. I wasn't the only person at this funeral luncheon who shouldn't be here. Rebecca might have seen Claire doing something suspicious, or she might have heard Claire say something that I missed because I was focused elsewhere.

I turned around. Rebecca was headed right for where Claire stood. We should have had a plan before we came here. I hadn't been taking this seriously enough. Could she have us arrested for trespassing? Technically we weren't mourners, which meant we hadn't been invited.

But there was no way she could have recognized Claire, and even though I could hear people talking now that the door was open, I could only pick out a few words. Claire wasn't stupid. She wouldn't have been yelling her questions.

Something else was happening.

I headed down the hallway after Rebecca. A man stood near Claire, a hat held in his hands. His frame was slightly boxy.

The hot air balloon operator.

Rebecca stopped in front of him and poked him in the chest with a manicured finger. I'd never seen someone actually do that except on TV.

"You have some nerve showing up here." Her voice was high-pitched to the point of sounding pulled thin.

He crushed his hat between both hands. "It wasn't my fault, what happened. The police believe me."

If he was telling the truth, that was the first I'd heard of it. Granted, Dan hadn't been around as much. The case had become high profile because of the strange circumstances. It wasn't every day that someone fell from a hot air balloon.

She put her finger back up to his chest and gave a little push. "You should never have taken him up in the balloon when he was sick. You should have known he might fall."

"I didn't even know he was sick." He held his hands up at chest level, a combination of *I surrender* and self-protection. "We needed to talk privately, and I needed to take off. My balloon seemed like the prefect place. How was I supposed to know he wouldn't be safe up there?"

Their conversation didn't make it clear whether they both knew the cause of death was an interaction with his medication. Rebecca sounded like she thought her husband had gotten dizzy or fainted and that's how he ended up falling over. The police could be holding back details so as not to tip their hand.

Rebecca covered her face, and her shoulders shook. An older woman with close-cropped silver hair, and a woman about my age who shared her nose and cheek bones, broke away from the crowd. The older woman put an arm around Rebecca and directed her out of the room, making shushing noises the whole time.

The hot air balloon operator watched them go. His face

sagged, as if that interaction hadn't gone the way he'd planned. Though what he expected to happen when he'd been a person of interest in Donald Wells' death, I wasn't sure.

He finally turned away, and our gazes met. His eyes narrowed in a way that made me think he was almost as unhappy to see me as Rebecca had been to see him.

The man who'd been talking to Rebecca in the kitchen stopped beside me, but he was facing the hot air balloon operator. "You need to leave."

I barely held back a reaction. He hadn't seemed to have much respect for his aunt, but he was still standing up for her as a member of the family and making sure no one upset her today. Or, at least, no one other than him.

He probably wouldn't be pleased if he knew the real reason Claire and I were there.

I edged backward. If Claire and I wanted to stay and find out anything more, I needed to be less visible right now. It was bad enough I'd interrupted Donald Wells' widow in the middle of a private conversation. I didn't need to be front and center when a person of interest was evicted from the wake.

The hot air balloon operator swung toward me. "If I have to leave because Don fell out of my balloon, then she should have to leave too. He ate a cupcake from her food truck right before he died. For all we know, she poisoned him and that's why he fell."

The conversations that had picked back up after Rebecca left the room fell into a hush again. The silence felt heavy enough even a forklift couldn't have moved it.

A hand wrapped around my elbow. Claire's vanilla and lavender perfume told me it was her.

"We've already been cleared by the police." Claire's voice held the distinct Claire confidence that brooked no further argument. "But since we've already paid our respects to the family, we'll be on our way."

She nodded to the man who'd asked the hot air balloon operator to leave and swept out the door with me in tow.

Once we were fifteen feet away, she leaned in. "Do you think that smoothed things over? The last thing our business needs is bad press. No one will hire us if they think we serve poisoned cupcakes."

7

The outlet store where I restocked my baking supplies locked their door behind me and shut off the lights at the front of the store. Outside, the sun had already set, leaving the parking lot illuminated by the anemic street lamp. Only the employees' cars were still in the lot.

And I'd forgotten to text Claire when I was checking out the way I was supposed to so that she could head out to pick me up. I'd gotten distracted by the size of the order I'd had to make. Thanks to the website my friend Eve created for me a few months ago, we'd gotten hired to create a display for the annual children's talent show. I couldn't understand why parents didn't just bring desserts the way they did for school events, but Claire said this was more like a mini-pageant. The winner would go on to compete at the state level.

The one benefit to the size of order I'd made this time was

they'd deliver. At least I wouldn't be trying to babysit a bunch of bags for however long it took Claire to reach me.

I texted her that I was done.

At the gym, her response said. *I thought you decided to walk home. I'll be about 20 minutes.*

Technically, since I didn't have bags to carry, I could walk home. It'd take about the same amount of time as waiting for Claire.

It was just that it was already dark.

I shivered even though it was still warm enough out that I didn't even need a light jacket. Neither choice was one I relished. I could stand here in the dark, probably well past when even the employees would have left. Or I could walk home in the dark.

When I was a little girl, my dad used to tell me there was nothing to fear in the dark that wasn't there in the daylight.

Maybe that was true. Maybe it wasn't. But at least in the daylight I could see the threats coming.

I gave myself a mental shake. This was silly. It was barely after nine, and the route back to Claire's house from here was mostly through the part of town that was restaurants and coffee shops. There'd be plenty of people.

I texted Claire back that it was a good night for a walk, and I'd meet her at home. That way she wouldn't have to rush her workout. Though, I thought she'd already been to the gym this morning.

No more stalling. Unless I wanted to huddle here until morning, waiting was only going to make my walk darker, not lighter. It wasn't like I'd never been out on the street after dark.

I left the hazy glow cast by the outlet store and headed toward home.

A sound like footsteps trailed behind me, and sweat burst out on my upper lip and forehead. My brain was bound to start playing tricks on me. It was probably just an employee headed for their car.

I glanced back over my shoulder. The natural darkness of the night and the shadows from the few light sources hid anyone who might or might not have been behind me. I couldn't hear the footsteps anymore.

Were the footsteps all in my head?

My skin felt like I'd walked through a cobweb and couldn't get all the strands off—sticky and shivery and imagining the worst. I picked up my pace. Not enough that someone following me would notice right away. Just enough to hopefully put a bit more space between us.

If Jarrod had found me at last, this was the worst possible situation to be in.

Strike that. The worst possible would be if he found me, and I was with Janie. This was the second worst. I was alone. I'd be dead before anyone knew he'd taken me.

The noise like footsteps started up behind me again. I wasn't a good enough judge of sound to tell if it was a man's or a woman's footfalls.

Dear God, let it be a woman. I'd be safe if it was a woman. A woman wouldn't want to hurt me. Besides, I could probably take a woman as long as she didn't have a gun. I was strong.

I lengthened my stride. If someone was following me, if Jarrod had found me, I needed to get to the strip of restaurants as quickly as possible. The lights ahead felt like the proverbial light at the end of the tunnel. They were close, but not close enough for anyone to help me if I screamed.

Screw it.

I broke into a jog. My purse bounced against my side, and I clutched it closer under one arm.

I couldn't hear if the person was still following me. My own breathing was too loud in my ears.

I ducked into the first establishment I reached, a coffee shop with only three tables. Two were full. I took the third.

The spot wasn't ideal. With how brightly lit the coffee shop was and how dark it was outside, the person who'd been following me could see I was in here. He could wait for me to come out.

Assuming anyone had actually been following me. I might have imagined it. Or I might not, but the footsteps might have belonged to someone innocently headed in the same direction. The hundred possible innocent explanations were all more likely than the one keeping me frozen to my seat—that Jarrod had found me at last.

Maybe my business was getting too big. I should never have

left the website up, even without my picture on it. The better known How Sweet It Is became, the more at risk I was.

I'd gotten too comfortable. Life had started to feel too easy. I'd started to think this could be my life permanently.

I sucked in a deep breath. Jumping to conclusions wouldn't help me. The footsteps had sounded real, but that didn't mean they were following me.

And yet, I couldn't walk the rest of the way home. That was too big a gamble.

I also couldn't call Claire. She was already stressed enough. The last thing I needed her thinking about was that my psychotic husband who could legally carry a concealed weapon might have found me. Neither of us would ever sleep again because she'd be up all night cleaning the house until she wore the floor to shreds.

Besides, it was embarrassing. This whole situation might be in my head.

If I was going to be humiliated, I was going to do it in front of one person and one person only. After all, he'd already seen me filthy and smelling like week-old hot garbage, literally.

I dialed Dan's number. The background sounded noisy when he answered even though I knew he wasn't at work. Janie always stayed with us when he had to work a late shift.

"Are you busy?" I asked.

"I'm with Janie at Tumble Bugs." He lowered his voice. "You saved me from the mom who's been flirting with me for the past two sessions. Talk as long as you want."

I'd forgotten tonight was Janie's gymnastics class. Maybe they could swing by and pick me up on their way home. I'd need to order a coffee soon anyway or the baristas would kick me out.

"That was a long pause." Dan's voice had lost its joking quality.

I swallowed hard, the combination of the dryness in my throat from my run and my pride making the words stick. "I need a ride." I explained the situation to him and how someone might or might not have been following me. "But I can wait."

"Where are you?" Dan asked.

I gave him the name of the coffee shop.

"That's less than five minutes from here. I'll pick you up and you can watch the rest of Janie's class with me. Janie will love it, and you'll save me from the barracuda mom."

I could imagine the single moms circling Dan. A laugh sneaked out before I could stop it, and I managed to keep it from ending on a sob. "Thank you."

"Wait inside for me. I'll come in."

I ordered us both a coffee in to-go cups and sat back down. Maybe I shouldn't have even hesitated to call him. He was the man who'd used the GPS tracker on my phone to find me when I wasn't answering, and he was worried for my safety. He'd also taken me seriously enough that he'd told me to wait inside.

My concern might be valid or it might have been all shadows and paranoia. But Dan hadn't made me feel like I was silly or a baby for being afraid. Somehow, being believed, being taken seriously instead of being told to relax, made all the difference. I could be calmer knowing he was on my side, whether there was a real threat or not.

Dan walked into the coffee shop door less than five minutes later. I handed him his coffee, and he placed a hand gently on my back as we exited the shop.

The touch sent spirals of sparks along my skin. It was a visual representation of him having my back. If someone was waiting for me to leave, they'd see I wasn't alone.

Dan opened the car door for me and climbed into the driver's side. He sipped his coffee as he drove away, but his gaze flickered to the rearview mirror. He switched lanes at the last minute and took a left turn even though Janie's gymnastics' studio was to the right.

He didn't say anything. Did he think I wouldn't notice that he was taking a circuitous route?

He glanced at the rear view mirror again and caught me watching him. "No one's following us."

I let out a sigh and slumped back into my seat. "Probably no one ever was."

Dan took another sip of coffee. "Better safe than sorry."

I closed my eyes. That was my life motto up until the past few months. "I forgot to think about Jarrod before I decided to walk."

Dan kept his eyes focused on the road as if he were trying to give me space. "That's healthy. You can't spend every moment of every day fixated on him."

I had, though. For so long that it'd felt normal. I couldn't remember when that had started to change, but it'd been some time after Dan, Janie, and Claire became a regular part of my life. It'd happened so slowly I hadn't even noticed. "It's stupid. But it's been nice to not feel afraid all the time." I tucked my hands between my knees. "I don't want to have to go back to being afraid all the time."

Dan slowed the car slightly. He glanced at me. "I'd like you to consider learning to defend yourself. It might have been Jarrod tonight. It might not. But you'll feel safer. And I'll worry about you less. All women should know self-defense."

I nodded. If I knew some techniques for stopping him or slowing him down if he did find me, I'd feel safer. Given how many murders I'd gotten tangled up in during the past year, knowing self-defense seemed like a useful skill even if Jarrod never found me.

"The department offers classes for free." Dan signaled and eased the car into a spot out front of Janie's gymnasium. "I could sign you up."

A class? No chance. A class gave Jarrod a routine he could track. "Can't I learn from a YouTube video or something?"

Dan chuckled. "It doesn't work that way. You didn't watch a YouTube video and suddenly you could decorate a cake, did you? You had to practice. Same thing."

He had a point. And maybe I'd passed the point where I needed to be concerned about a pattern where someone could watch me and know where I'd be. I lived in a house now, not a truck where I parked somewhere different each night. Someone didn't have to watch me and learn a pattern. They only had to follow me home.

Anything was worth trying if it meant I could be less afraid. "Okay. Sign me up."

8

*T*he sign on the door of the fitness center told me I was at the right place. Women's self-defense class from 6:00 to 8:00 pm. Open to anyone. It gave a number where women interested in joining were supposed to call and sign up.

"Is the door locked?" a petite blonde about the same height as my friend Eve asked.

I hadn't even tried the door yet. How long had I been standing here reading and re-reading the sign? Maybe I should have asked Eve to join me. Or even Claire. Then I might not feel like my feet had grown roots.

The blonde woman rapped on the glass door rather than waiting for me to answer. A burly man wearing a Lakeshore Police Department t-shirt opened it for us. He had to be at least six feet tall, and the shirt stretched tight across his muscles.

The blonde thanked him and ducked inside. She didn't even

seem to care that she had to squeeze by him.

He looked down at me. He probably didn't mean for the tilt of his chin and lack of a smile to be intimidating.

"Are you here for the class?" His tone held the welcome his expression lacked.

But if this man was the instructor, did that mean I'd have to grapple with him to practice? Somehow I'd expected the class to be led by a woman. That'd been naïve of me. A female would likely help him demonstrate the things taught in class, but we'd need male instructors for there to be any sort of practical application.

I hadn't thought this through.

Little black curlicues swam at the edge of my vision.

My phone rang in my pocket. I grabbed it out and held it up like a shield. "I have to get this first."

He nodded but something in the way he moved made me think he didn't believe me. "Door'll be unlocked for you."

I slid my finger across the screen without even glancing at the number. "How Sweet It Is Cupcakes. Isabel speaking."

"Good evening, Isabel." The man's voice on the other end of the line was slow and smooth and vaguely familiar. "I'm sorry to call at dinner time, but I assume businesses like yours are probably open for the dinner rush."

I made an affirmative noise. The man's approach made me think we'd met before. Cold call customers weren't usually so familiar.

"This is Elijah Wells. You gave me your card at my uncle's funeral."

The conversation between Elijah and Rebecca leapt back into my mind. Rebecca had no reason to murder her husband. She lost her style of living upon his death. Elijah, on the other hand, had a good motive if he resented Rebecca living off his uncle's wealth and wanted it returned to the family.

He cleared his throat softly as if my pause had been long enough to become awkward.

I switched my phone to the other ear. "I remember you. I didn't think you'd actually use my card once we left the way we did."

He chuckled softly in a way that sounded kind. "I don't believe you poisoned my uncle if that's what you mean. Quite the opposite. I'd like to do a tasting and discuss options for supplying my business on a weekly basis. You didn't list an address on your business card or I would have simply stopped by."

His speech had a formal quality to it that reminded me of someone who'd traveled to so many locations around the world that the influence of all the different accents came together to make his speech stiffer than the average.

I couldn't tell him that we didn't have a physical location. We'd sound like small fries. He might decide to find a more established business to work with, regardless of how much he enjoyed my cupcakes. I needed to stall him so I could think.

"What did you have in mind?"

"Right now, when we have clients in, all we have to offer them is stale croissants and bland muffins. My uncle thought that was good enough. He didn't understand that the current competitive climate means we need to woo our clients. I want to give them something they can't get from just anywhere. I want to show them that we care about their business."

He rattled off the number of cupcakes they'd want on average each week.

The contract was exactly the kind of thing that gave a catering business stability. I had a few of them, and they'd made all the difference.

If only this offer wasn't coming from someone who had a motive for murder. Everything he'd said about his uncle only strengthened his motive. From the sounds of it, he'd taken over his uncle's spot in the family business, and he'd also obviously felt for a long time that he had better ideas. Ideas his uncle refused to listen to. Financial gain or saving a business that someone truly cared about were both potential motives for murder.

I couldn't meet with him in my truck alone. I wasn't stupid enough to take that risk, even if I had been brave enough to be alone with a strange man—which I wasn't. Unfortunately, there wasn't room for three of us to do a tasting in there. When I'd done my friend Nicole's wedding tasting, we'd both barely fit, and that was in my larger truck.

I also couldn't turn down a regular contract when I didn't

have solid evidence that he was the one who murdered his uncle. Sabotaging our business on a suspicion was short-term thinking. He, Claire, and I would have to meet at the house. Not that giving our address to a potential murderer ranked high on the list of safe things to do, but what other option did we have?

Besides, Claire would never forgive me if I passed up this opportunity. Not only would it help our business, but it'd also give us a chance to find out more about Donald Wells and why someone might have wanted him dead.

If Elijah hadn't done it, he'd make a fantastic source of information down the line. Once we had a working relationship, we'd be able to slip in a few questions here and there. We'd even have a chance to observe Donald Wells' business a bit more and see if anyone there might have had a motive other than Elijah.

"Let me check dates with my partner," I said, "and I'll get back to you."

He confirmed that the phone number he'd called from was the best one to reach him on. We disconnected the call.

I turned back to the gym door, and my stomach felt like a clump of tangled string.

I couldn't go in yet. First, I should text Claire. I sent her a message and then watched my screen for the dots that would signal she was writing back. Nothing. She was probably in the pool at her gym tonight. She wouldn't be expecting to hear from me until 8:15 when I was supposed to pick her up.

This was important. Maybe I should drive there and talk to her now instead of waiting.

That's an excuse, Fear whispered in my ear.

That was great. Fear agreed with Dan that I should learn to defend myself.

I pinched the bridge of my nose. They were both right. Learning to defend myself could buy me the precious seconds I needed to get away if I was attacked. Jarrod might never find me, but all the murders I'd seen had proved one thing. The world was full of evil people.

But the self-defense class wasn't going to do me any good if I couldn't even find the courage to step inside, let alone have the instructor touch me. Dan had made it clear that I couldn't learn self-defense by watching. I needed to learn by doing.

If doing involved a man touching me, then I had only one option.

I dialed Dan's number. He picked up after a couple of rings.

"You're not being followed again, are you? I thought you were going to the self-defense class tonight."

The tension in his voice cut straight through to the fortress where I'd tried to lock my heart. I mattered to him. It was an odd feeling to know your well-being mattered that much to another human being. I knew he'd agree to my request even before I asked.

"I couldn't do it. Will you teach me instead?"

9

"We have this room for the two hours," Dan said as he opened the door for me. "And we'll only be able to do our sessions when the common session is running. That's when the department has the gym reserved."

I nodded. I'd wanted him to teach me at his house or Claire's, but he'd insisted that we needed floors with better padding so neither of us ended up breaking something.

Matching the time slot of the regular self-defense session meant we might not even be able to practice each week if Dan had to work or couldn't convince one of the relatives to babysit Janie. But I was willing to make concessions and take it slow if it meant he'd teach me rather than some stranger.

Dan had tried to convince me the police detective running the class was a teddy bear and one of the nicest guys I'd ever meet. Apparently, the burly instructor's name was Zee, and he was one of Dan's best friends. That knowledge still wasn't enough to make me feel brave enough to go to the class. Dan explained to Zee that I was an abuse survivor, and Zee helped us get permission to hold our private lessons at the same time.

I turned in a slow circle. The room was clearly used for exercise classes at other times. Yoga mats lay rolled and piled in one corner, and exercise balls and hand weights lined the walls. The floor under my feet was squishy enough that I wasn't even sure why people would need the yoga mats.

Dan stepped in front of me and waited until I met his gaze. "I can't be gentle with you once we start practicing. You'll have some bruises."

Intellectually I knew that. The tension that radiated through my entire body, making my back muscles spasm, told a different story. I forced what I hoped was a brave smile. "All in the pursuit of safety."

The image of Rebecca accusing the hot air balloon operator at the funeral flashed into my mind. Since no one else was in the balloon with them, there was no way of knowing what had actually happened, but maybe there were some clues still. Like bruises.

I wasn't going to be able to concentrate on Dan's lesson with that floating around in my mind. "Can I ask you an unrelated question first?"

Dan straightened from tightening his shoelace. "The fact that you felt you need to ask if you can ask tells me I might not like this, but go ahead."

"Claire and I went to the funeral for Donald Wells. The hot air balloon operator showed up, and Wells' widow seemed to feel he was responsible for Wells' death. What you just said got me thinking. Were there any signs that the operator tried to stop Wells from jumping?"

The look he gave me said he knew he had to give me some answer or my mind would be divided. If I couldn't focus, I'd have wasted both our time.

He shook his head. "No signs of a struggle. No signs of defensive wounds or what you'd expect to see if he were trying to stop Wells from jumping out. But you have to remember that he might have been afraid of being pushed over the side himself."

That was true. There was a reason not everyone went into a career in the military or as a first responder. Those people had to put their lives in jeopardy to protect others. Most people's self-preservation instincts were high enough that they couldn't bring themselves to do it. The hot air balloon operator might have tried to stop Wells verbally, but he might not have felt comfortable trying to stop him physically.

So we were still at square one. Time to focus on what I was here for. "So where do we start?"

Dan moved close enough that he could have touched me, but he kept his arms by his sides. "Let's start with something simple. What to do if someone tries to choke you from behind." He motioned for me to spin around so that my back was to him. "I'm going to do this slow. I want you to drop your chin as soon as you feel motion behind you."

He slid an arm around my waist. His other arm came up.

My brain shouted for me to drop my chin, but my head wouldn't move. My whole body felt like it'd been encased in ice. The phantom of Jarrod, his thumbs crushing my windpipe, flamed across my vision.

The next thing I knew, I was sitting on the floor, my head between my knees, and Dan was telling me to breath in and out to his count. He wasn't touching me at all anymore.

Why had I thought this would be okay with Dan? Just because he'd held my hand before when we were pretending to be dating to investigate a lead in the last murder case I helped with. Just because we danced together in the rain once. Just because I was okay touching his arm.

I was too broken. He was going to see that I was too broken to be around his family.

"Are you breathing a little easier?" Dan asked softly.

I nodded. My tongue still felt seared and unwieldy.

"I'm so sorry. I didn't realize."

I shook my head. I couldn't listen to him give up on me too. "Talk to me about something else for a minute."

He'd been kneeling beside me. He sat on the floor next to me, his legs partially pulled up, so he could rest his arms across them. He'd left well over a foot between us. "Like about how you and

Claire probably weren't at that funeral just to mourn a man you'd met once for less than five minutes."

His tone was light. It lifted away a layer of the heaviness that pinned me to the floor. "Something other than lecturing me about staying out of this case." I tried to match his tone. My voice came out reedy. "What were Donald Wells and the hot air balloon operator arguing about?"

My ragged breathing filled the quiet gap that settled between us.

Dan shifted. "I'm only telling you this because I don't want either of you putting yourselves in a dangerous situation trying to find out."

I nodded my understanding.

"Andy Frank and Donald Wells were childhood friends. They'd grown apart as they got older, but Frank says he saw Wells' wife going into a lawyer's office. He'd been blindsided by a divorce recently himself, and he didn't want that for his friend."

My mind cleared slightly. That didn't fit with what I heard at the funeral luncheon. I gathered the pieces of myself and sat up. "Either Andy Frank is lying or Rebecca Wells was going to a lawyer about something else. I overheard her talking with one of the other family members at the funeral. Whatever she got from his death was a lot less than what she got from being married to him. My guess is her prenup was even tighter, and she wouldn't have gotten anything in a divorce."

"That's what I thought as well. The rest of the team assigned to this case isn't looking at Frank as a suspect anymore, but I think we've moved on too soon. When I spoke to Mrs. Wells, she insisted she hadn't been to a lawyer in years. One of them is lying. Just because Frank didn't push Donald Wells out of the hot air balloon doesn't mean he might not have found a way to give him the lime juice that resulted in his death."

My legs felt much steadier than they had before. The distraction of talking about the case had worked. I eased to my feet. "I'm sorry for wasting your time."

Dan hoped up and brushed off his pants. "Ready to try again? I'll go slower this time. We'll start with just my hands on your shoulders."

His stance was loose, like he didn't think anything of what he'd just said.

My heart felt tight in my chest. "You're not giving up on me?"

He smiled in that way that sent crinkles out from the corners of his eyes. "Never."

10

*E*lijah Wells was so prompt it was almost painful.

The doorbell rang just as the clock ticked over to the time set for our meeting. He was probably the kind of person who arrived somewhere early but stayed in his car to be sure to be on time without inconveniencing the other person by being early.

I smoothed down my apron.

Claire opened the door. "Thanks again for meeting here. We're still trying to settle on a retail location. It's not an easy choice."

The lie was a small one, but neither of us had wanted to admit to a new client that our entire business was a loaner food truck. Over time, this contract could make up for the loss we'd taken when the hot air balloon festival shut down and only reopened for the final day. We needed to nail it.

Elijah stepped inside and shook both our hands.

I hadn't paid much attention to him when I'd spoken to him briefly at the funeral. He didn't look like his uncle except for his dark hair and golden quality of his skin. He was taller than his uncle had been—at least from what I remembered—with a neatly trimmed goatee that made his jaw look even more square. He wore a three-piece suit even though it was Saturday afternoon.

Claire and I looked underdressed in comparison. We'd opted for the matching pink and purple How Sweet It Is t-shirts she bought us earlier in the summer when we'd catered the annual barbecue for an insurance company. We'd added the aprons because Claire thought they gave us a more professional look. At least we were dressed befitting out job.

"We've laid out a selection of sweet and savory," Claire said, "based on what you told Isabel you were looking for."

Had I not known this was Claire's first time liaising with a client, I wouldn't have known. She sounded like she'd done this so many times she could have repeated her lines under sedation. Coming across with confidence was definitely one of her strengths.

We'd made the kitchen look as professional as possible with a table cloth that matched the business colors. Elijah waited for us to take our seats as if he were an old-fashioned gentleman rather than a man in his early forties.

I laid out the first round of samples. "We have a few ways we can do a regular delivery like this depending on your budget."

I explained the options to him. Claire hovered by my shoulder the whole time as if she wanted to say something but knew it'd look bad if she cut me off. I stumbled over my words a couple of times. It was like trying to write a test in school with the teacher staring at every word you wrote.

I finished, and Claire put another cupcake onto Elijah's plate. "This is the variety Isabel made for your uncle's funeral, so you might already have tasted it, but it's always good to have a comparison."

Elijah accepted the cupcake and cut into it with the knife we provided. "I thought I recognized you from the luncheon as well."

Claire slid into her chair and shifted it ever so slightly closer to him. "We wanted to give our respects even though we'd only met him once. It seemed like the right thing to do."

Elijah smiled in a way that could have been genuine or could have been someone who'd trained for a long time to make sure fake smiles looked genuine. "I appreciate that."

Claire looked like she considered patting his hand and then thought better of it.

Was she flirting? Elijah was my age. She was closer to Donald Wells' age.

"We were sorry for the disturbance when Mr. Frank showed up. We didn't realize he'd have a problem with us being there."

The softness around Elijah's eyes tightened. "Mr. Frank overstepped. He had no right to request anyone leave my uncle's house."

His uncle's house. Not his aunt's house or even Rebecca's house. That confirmed what I'd overheard that the house didn't belong to her now that her husband had died. This had to be difficult for her. Donald Wells' family didn't seem to feel much sympathy for her either.

If Claire was trying to smooth over the scene at the funeral, she was going about it the wrong way. Besides, she didn't need to smooth anything over. He'd come to us even after what happened at the funeral luncheon. All we had to do was impress him with our food. This wasn't like Claire.

I handed him the sheet I'd made with all the options listed. "As you're testing each, you can mark down whether it's something you'd like us to bring to you or not. There's also a spot at the bottom where you can include any allergies or other restrictions. We know some buildings are nut-free."

The hard edges forming around his eyes softened again. "That's very thoughtful. One of the reasons I hoped you'd be a good fit for working with our company, even in this capacity, was the kindness you showed by bringing something to the funeral luncheon. I see my instincts were correct."

So my ignorance about social customs had actually gotten us this opportunity. In a small way, it reminded me of the story of Ruth in the Bible. Ruth was a widow who ended up re-married to a good man because she was out gleaning wheat in a field and accidentally drew attention to herself. God used many unusual circumstances for his plan.

Maybe someday I'd be able to look at everything that had happened to me and feel the same way about all of it. Maybe.

"I've never been great with words," I said, "but I can speak with food."

He grinned at me in a way that I knew was genuine this time even if I couldn't have said how I knew. Objectively, his expression looked the same as before. "That you can."

"Does the hot air balloon operator have a history with your family?" Claire's voice was a little too casual. "Mrs. Wells didn't seem happy to see him, and it seemed like her dislike ran deeper than what happened."

My stomach torqued. Oh no. That's what Claire was playing at. She wasn't flirting. She wasn't trying to ingratiate us. She was trying to dig for information on the case.

This wasn't the time for that. I wanted to figure out who killed Donald Wells too. And I wasn't naïve. I knew that no matter how nice Elijah seemed, he could be the murderer. But he wasn't likely to give up anything useful to us right now. If we landed this job, we'd have more interactions with him where we could learn things that might be important.

Not only that, but Claire's approach was about as subtle as a truck driving into the side of a building. He struck me as someone who was too savvy to slip up with such blatant interrogation techniques.

I snapped up his water glass and shoved it into Claire's hand even though it was only half full. "Let us refill that for you. You still have a few to get through."

He gave the same smile as before, where his lips looked softer. "It's a good thing I skipped lunch."

Something about his smile made me want to return it.

Remember, Fear whispered, *evil hides behind handsome faces and warm smiles.*

I imagined shoving Fear into a box and locking the lid. Evil did hide in those places, but as Dan liked to remind me, if I refused to trust anyone at all, I'd have a very empty life.

I wasn't going to trust Elijah yet, but I also wasn't going to treat him like a confirmed murderer. For now, I was going to treat him like an honored customer.

I smiled back at him. "I fully advocate eating cupcakes for at least two meals of the day."

Claire set the cup on water back on the table beside him. The look she gave him, eyebrows up and gaze unwavering, said she was still waiting for the answer to her question. When Janie or I faced that look, we caved.

Elijah returned her look calmly. "Rebecca, my uncle's wife, was quite distraught at the funeral, as you might imagine. In times of tragedy, we all look for a reason or someone to blame. I don't think she truly suspects Mr. Frank any more than she suspects you."

The implication was clear to me at least. Claire's poking

around was suspicious to him. He probably didn't think she had anything to do with killing his uncle, but he might have caught on to what she was doing. Or perhaps he did suspect us. What better way to see if we might have been involved in slipping the lime juice to his uncle than to hire us, so he'd have an excuse to check us out.

"Surely you must suspect someone, though," Claire said.

I wanted to hide my face. Claire had a lot of good qualities. She was a wiz at organization. She could take command of a situation and get things done. She was determined. But tact and subtlety were not among her positive attributes.

Elijah rose to his feet. "I must be going. Do you mind if I return this slip to you once I've had time to consider the options?"

He addressed the question to me.

I bowed my head slightly in acknowledgment. "Let me walk you out."

Claire looked like she was either going to point out that he hadn't tried everything yet or invite herself to join us on the walk out. I glared at her. She glared back but gathered up the remains of the tasting.

I trailed behind Elijah out of the house. Social niceties weren't my area of expertise. I wasn't sure whether to pretend like it hadn't happened. Even if we got the job now, he'd be on his guard against future questions.

Pretending like it hadn't happened didn't seem like the right path, whether we got the job or not. Elijah had come to this tasting in good faith—as far as I knew—and he'd been ambushed.

"I'm sorry for my business partner," I said quietly. "She's been struggling ever since she saw your uncle fall."

He stopped beside his car and turned back to face me. "I don't blame her. I wasn't even there, and I've been having nightmares about it." He pressed his key fob, and his car beeped. "But I hope you'll understand if part of the agreement should we offer you this contract is that you be the one to deliver the goods."

I bobbed my head. "Of course."

He climbed into his car. "I'll be in touch."

He pulled away. The adrenaline left my body, and I wanted to slump down into the grass and sit there for a few minutes. Instead, I forced myself to go back inside.

Claire stood next to the front door, her hands on her hips. "Why did you keep blocking me? This was the perfect opportunity to get more information on the case."

The part of me that had been conditioned to back away from confrontation shrunk inside me. But I couldn't let it win. Not this time. Claire was my business partner and my roommate. On top of that, I'd worked too hard to save and keep my business to let anything happen to it now.

"He knew what you were doing. He wasn't going to give us any information, and we were at risk of losing the job."

My words didn't come out as forceful as I'd hoped. If I was

being honest with myself, they weren't forceful at all. More like a squeak than a thundercloud.

Claire pursed her lips, and her hands tightened on her hips. "There's no need to exaggerate."

Her voice carried the tiniest hesitation. Had I not spent so much time with her lately, I wouldn't have heard it.

"I wish I was exaggerating." This time I kept my voice soft on purpose.

Claire huffed out a breath. "I'm not cut out for investigating. Dan managed to go undercover multiple times. I don't understand it. Getting information out of people without them knowing it is a lot harder than it looks on TV." She glanced at the door. "Do you think we still have a chance at the contract?"

"I'm only guessing, but he seemed like he might be willing to overlook it as long as we didn't make a habit of poking into his family's personal lives."

Claire jutted her chin toward the kitchen. "I've been going to the gym enough lately. I think we should finish the rest of the tasting menu for supper."

I couldn't have come up with a better idea myself.

11

*T*he security guard at the front door of the building checked that my name was on a list of approved visitors and then gave me directions to find Elijah's office. I wasn't sure exactly what his business was other than it was something in the financial sector, but the building was open and bright. Everyone in it seemed to speak so softly that my footsteps sounded like I was stomping.

When Elijah called to give us the contract, he'd actually apologized for making us wait one day. I'd heard women talk about men waiting longer than that to call after a great first date.

I reached the third floor, and a woman waved to me from behind an open desk. Her red-hair was pulled back neatly into a bun.

"I'm Mr. Wells' assistant." She waved me in like I was a kid late for class. "Mr. Wells office is straight ahead. Go right in. He's waiting for you." She winked at me as I passed. "I'm so glad you're saving us from those dry pastries we've been subjected to until now."

Her approach made me feel like she'd have invited me for a cup of tea if I didn't have an appointment already. Whatever type of financial work this office did, they didn't strike me as the typical stuffy office environment.

I knocked softly on Elijah's door and went inside.

He rose to his feet. "Just in time. Mary Ellen has been worried you wouldn't get here before the Every Child's Wish people, even though they're not coming until this afternoon."

Every Child's Wish was a Michigan organization that did something similar to the national Make-A-Wish Foundation. Their scope was a little broader. They granted the wishes of terminally-ill children, but they also set up entertainment and other joy-bringing events for children's floors at hospitals. I'd read about them in the Positivity Project column.

I carefully set the cupcake boxes down on the edge of his desk. "I didn't know charities would have money to invest."

Elijah moved around his desk and opened the lid of the top cupcake box as if he couldn't help himself. He smiled gently and covered them again. "I don't know whether they'd need our services or not. They're coming because we want to set up a regular donor arrangement. The type of thing where we meet their needs, and they display our logo along with their other major donors."

My face felt numb, like I couldn't smile or raise my eyebrows because my brain didn't know which reaction to pick. That was the last thing I'd been expecting. Financial companies didn't have a reputation for generosity. They had a reputation for being cutthroat and, sometimes, for gambling with money that people could ill afford to lose.

Elijah chuckled, a soft noise that reminded me of the relaxing sound of leaves rustling. "My family has always had a philanthropic mindset. Making a lot of money isn't just about us. It's about having enough that we can donate at a level that will make a difference for important charities."

The fact that the family wasn't willing to let Rebecca Wells live off of Donald's money now made more sense. They believed in working for their own comfort but also for filling needs outside the family.

It wasn't a mentality that was common anymore. Even politicians and other advocates who were the most vocal about charities and needs didn't seem to put their own money into those causes. It always confused me when I saw athletes using their celebrity to make political and social statements but keeping their millions in their own bank accounts. What did a person even do with millions of dollars anyway?

Elijah seemed to be someone who actually did something to better the world. I didn't want him to be the one who killed his uncle. No doubt if he was, he'd have believed his motives were noble. But Elijah seemed like a genuinely nice human being. I needed some people in the world to just be good people, to just be what they seemed. Dan was that way, and he felt like too rare a person.

I touched the top of the cupcake boxes. "The cardboard is recyclable. Let me know by Wednesday what flavors you'd like for next Friday. Are you meeting with a charity that saves puppies then?"

Elijah shook his head. "Unfortunately, not, though perhaps I'll have Mary Ellen gather information on the Michigan Humane Society."

Dan would have teased that puppies were next month. Elijah's serious response almost made me feel irreverent for my joke.

I backed toward the door. "Thanks for giving us a chance."

If I hadn't still been facing him, I would have flinched. That sounded desperate.

Elijah's soft smile spread across his face again. "My staff is thanking you."

I clicked the door shut behind me, but Mary Ellen was already headed toward the door. Her smile was bright enough it could have lit up a stadium.

She ducked into the room and came back out with the boxes, closing the door behind her again. "Mr. Wells had nothing but good things to say about your cupcakes. I can barely wait for the meeting to try them."

She disappeared down the hall.

Maybe this place was too good to be true. It felt a bit like walking on rainbows and sunshine. Everyone was cheerful and peaceful, and they gave away money. It could be the business version of *The Stepford Wives*.

Or maybe I was just a cynic.

I headed back in the direction I'd come from. A woman's voice hissed out of a partially opened door in front of me. I stopped. Not all unicorn sparkles after all.

"You need to leave me alone," the woman's voice said.

Not any woman. The voice either belonged to Rebecca Wells or someone who could have done an amazing imitation of her.

First she'd blasted Andy Frank at the funeral, believing he'd either killed her husband or had negligently taken him up in the hot air balloon even though he was obviously ill.

Now she'd come to her husband's former place of business and was accosting the employees. She seemed to lack a sense of timing or discretion.

Or perhaps that was how she handled grief. Grief could make people do things and say things they'd never have thought possible. Especially if they were looking for a reason or someone to blame, as Elijah had said.

When my dad died, I hadn't blamed the doctors, which might have been the natural thing to do. My dad died from an interaction between his weak heart and an allergic reaction. Instead, I'd blamed myself. If I hadn't taken us on that picnic. If I had worked extra shifts, so we could have seen another specialist. If. If. If.

Looking back, carrying around that self-loathing might have been part of what contributed to making me an easy target for Jarrod.

"I don't understand, Becca." The man's voice from inside the office snapped me back into the present. "You had no problem being with me while your husband was alive. Now that he's gone, you want to break things off. That's backwards."

I should *not* be listening to this conversation. Rebecca Wells would not be forgiving if she caught me accidentally eavesdropping on her a second time.

I glanced over my shoulder. Unless I wanted to go back into Elijah's office or into one of the meeting rooms, there wasn't a way out in that direction. Reaching the stairs or elevator required me to pass by the door and potentially be spotted.

"I don't expect you to understand," Rebecca said. "I do expect you to respect my decision."

"Don't do this, baby." The man's voice turned low and sultry. Heat crept up my neck just listening to it. "We can be together guilt-free now. That's all we ever wanted."

Rebecca made a noise that sounded like she was either choking or crying. "Not guilt free."

The door swung open, and Rebecca sailed out. I jumped backward, but she didn't look in my direction at all. I stayed as still as possible just in case.

Rebecca might not have had a reason to murder her husband, but her boyfriend did. He'd sounded convinced that Donald's death fixed everything. They'd wanted to be together openly, but Rebecca either couldn't or wouldn't leave Donald. Now Donald was dead, they could be together, and they didn't have to sneak around or feel bad anymore.

Not that the boyfriend sounded like he felt bad even when they'd been sneaking around. He'd sounded more like he was glad Rebecca wouldn't have to feel bad anymore.

The boyfriend's motive might even have gone deeper than that. He couldn't have known Rebecca would break up with him after her husband's death. Perhaps he assumed she'd marry him if he asked. He'd probably expected Rebecca would inherit Donald Wells' wealth, and he would get both Rebecca and the money with Donald gone.

Even if the money hadn't factored in, if she refused to leave her husband because she knew about the will, her secret boyfriend could have seen killing Donald as a way to free her.

Based on the conversation I'd overheard, Rebecca might have been close to breaking it off with her secret boyfriend before her husband died. Now she couldn't stand to continue, knowing that she'd been unfaithful to her husband while he was alive. If her boyfriend had killed for her, that could put her life at risk too once he realized he wasn't going to be able to win her back.

I needed to get a little closer so I could read the name on his door. Dan and the others investigating Donald Wells' death might not know about him. If they'd been able to keep their affair a secret from Donald, there probably wouldn't be a record for the police to follow either.

I moved forward. The name plate on the door said *Leon Schwab*.

Before my eyes could register his title, a man's form filled the doorway. He didn't look anything like a Leon. He didn't look anything like Donald Wells either. He had the kind of face that could have landed him a role as one of the doctors on *Grey's Anatomy* that showed up in all the "steamy" and "dreamy" memes online. I'd never watched the show, so I didn't know their names, but I saw the appeal. He was also closer to Rebecca's age than Donald Wells had been.

His hand on the doorknob suggested he'd come to close the door. "Who are you? What are you doing on this floor?"

Great. The last thing I needed was for him to remember my face.

I ducked my head. "I was here for a delivery, and I was looking for the bathroom. Clearly this isn't it."

He hooked a thumb in the direction of the stairs. "It's that way. The one with the picture of the person wearing the skirt."

He crossed his arms and leaned against the door frame. Part of him clearly didn't believe my story, and he was going to watch to make sure I actually did go into the bathroom rather than entering a different office.

I thanked him as if I hadn't heard the snark in his answer and ducked through the door that was clearly marked as a woman's washroom. I walked over to the nearest sink and leaned on it.

My blood pumped hard through my body. Every part of me felt a little wobbly.

One of the stall doors opened, but the person inside didn't move to one of the sinks.

"Are you stalking me?"

12

*M*y gaze met Rebecca Wells' in the bathroom mirror. I turned around slowly.

Based on the smudges of mascara still lingering under her eyes, she'd been crying and had tried to fix her make-up before going into the bathroom stall. The lights in the bathroom gave her skin a washed-out appearance. She might not have been as young as I originally thought when I saw her at the funeral. Donald Wells was in his sixties. Rebecca Wells could have been in her early fifties.

That created another strange age gap, though, if she was. Her boyfriend couldn't have been more than mid-forties.

She lifted one drawn-in eyebrow at me. "Well?"

I stuck my hands behind me and gripped the edge of the sink. Rebecca wasn't going to hurt me, but I felt trapped. "I was delivering cupcakes."

"Both here and at my husband's funeral?" She swept to the other sink and twisted the handle so forcefully I thought it might fly off. She pumped more soap into her palm than any one person could actually need. "My husband's dead. Isn't that enough? There's nothing left to investigate. Why can't you just leave me alone now?"

Nothing left to investigate? That made it sound like she suspected someone was following her or having her followed. Maybe to find evidence of her affair?

No, that didn't make sense. She'd sounded like her husband being dead should have closed the investigation because it involved him rather than her. If someone had been investigating Donald Wells before he died, then he might have been killed over something he was doing.

Fortunately or unfortunately, that opened up the suspect pool. It could have still been Rebecca's boyfriend but with the added motive of rescuing her from whatever trouble Donald had gotten them into. As much as I hated to think it, it could be Elijah as well. Donald might have been doing something that would put the business in jeopardy.

But if someone was following Rebecca and thought she might lead them to something, it was more likely personal—something Donald was involved in apart from the family business.

Without more to go on, all I had were guesses.

I stayed still. Staying very still tended to make a person seem less threatening. "I've heard a lot of good things about your husband. If you think something I've heard isn't true, good or bad, I'd be grateful if you corrected me."

She shut the water off and flicked droplets off her hands into the sink. "Do you think I'm stupid?" She glanced at me. "Private investigator?"

She clearly wasn't going to tell me anything if she thought that was the case. "Cupcake baker."

She made a mm-hmm noise. She blasted her hands under the hand dryer. When it shut off, she stepped one step closer to me. "A reporter then?" She glanced in the mirror and swiped a finger underneath one eye. "If I didn't give an interview to the Michigan Daily for more than you probably make in a year, I'm not going to give one to whatever slimy little paper you belong to." She narrowed her eyes. "And if I see you following me again, I'm calling the police and getting a restraining order."

Could she do that? I wasn't actually following her around. But it wouldn't matter if I was or I wasn't. If she called the police and accused me of it, the police might dig into who I was. I took out one of my business cards and handed it to her. "I really am a baker. I was hired here because of the cupcakes I brought to your husband's funeral."

Rebecca glanced at it and sniffed. "Pirate."

"Do you meant privateer? A pirate steals things. A privateer is more like a mercenary. They take advantage of situations for their own profit."

She brushed past me and out the door.

"Nice, Isabel," I whispered to myself. "You really made a friend by correcting her English."

My dad and I used to joke that one of the side effects of having a father who was an English teacher was that I grew up with an inherited pet peeve for grammatical mistakes and misused words. It'd never won me any friends.

Hopefully Rebecca's boyfriend—ex-boyfriend now—wasn't still watching the ladies' room door, but just in case he was, I'd take my time. I headed into the nearest stall.

A woman's purse hung on the hook on the back of the door.

It had to be Rebecca's purse. This was the stall she'd come out of.

I slid it off the hook and paused. Should I chase after her and try to return her purse?

I held it in my hands. She hadn't even zipped it up. I could see the contents.

It wouldn't take long for me to look through what was inside. Claire had been up again cleaning last night. I heard her scrubbing down the bathroom—the guest bathroom that was my responsibility to clean since I was the one using it. When I asked her what she was doing, she'd said it was better than lying in bed and thinking about how the person who'd killed Donald Wells was still free.

Who knew what I might find in Rebecca's purse that could help this case? Maybe she'd kept the business card of the reporter who contacted her for an interview. With a name and phone number, the police could try to find out what story the reporter wanted to write. That could generate a lead on who else might have had motive.

My chest felt heavy. If I rummaged through her purse, I'd be no better than what she'd accused me of. I might not be a private investigator or a reporter, but if I went into her purse, I'd be invading her privacy.

I could use Claire as a justification, but Claire wouldn't want me to. Dan wouldn't either. A few months ago, that wouldn't have mattered to me, but their opinions mattered now. They'd given me the benefit of the doubt so many times. They'd put themselves on the line to protect me.

They wouldn't want me to turn into a criminal, no matter how small the crime.

If I hurried, I might still be able to catch Rebecca and return her purse before she left the building. I looped her purse over my wrist.

I hustled toward the door and reached for the handle. The door swung in. It cracked into my hand. Pain flared through my knuckles, and Rebecca's purse flipped into the air. Her purse hit the floor, and the contents gushed out like yolk from a cracked egg.

I dropped down beside it.

High-heeled feet stopped beside me. One foot tapped on the

floor. "What are you doing with my purse? Did you dump it out so you could paw through it?"

I ran my gaze up until I met Rebecca's glare leveled down at me. Somehow I doubted she'd believe me if I told her the truth. "It was an accident. Let me help you clean it up."

"Sure it was an accident. Sure it was." Rebecca's mouth twisted as if I'd asked her to eat a raw snake. "My belongings are all over the filthy bathroom floor. I don't see how that could be accidental. My phone!"

She squatted just long enough to swipe her phone off the floor.

If I'd ever hoped to be able to ask this woman questions that might help figure out who had killed her husband, I certainly wasn't going to be able to now. I'd be lucky if she didn't want to report me for attempted purse nabbing. That was definitely a crime.

Rebecca tapped at her screen with a fingernail that was too long to be natural. "I think that's a crack. You cracked my screen."

I could only pray that wasn't true. Her phone looked like the newest model. It probably cost a few thousand dollars. I couldn't possibly replace it.

I grabbed up a handful of scribbled notes and receipts. "I'll help you clean it up. I promise it was an accident. I was coming to return it to you when you opened the door and hit my hands."

"Oh so it's my fault." Her voice went impossibly shrill. "I see how it is."

She snagged her partially filled purse, pivoted on her heel, and left me standing with the handful of papers. I collected the last few off the floor. All I could do was go after her and try to give them back.

I hurried out of the bathroom and looked automatically toward the direction of the stairs and elevator. Rebecca wasn't there. I slowly turned in the other direction.

Leon, Mary Ellen, and another employee I hadn't seen before all stood inside the hallway next to the doors to the rooms they must have been in. Rebecca stood with Elijah by his office door.

Not good. Not good at all. I should have known Rebecca wouldn't let this go, especially if her phone was broken.

I glanced down at the paper scraps and receipts in my hand. Would it look more incriminating to try to give them back to her or to simply stuff them in my own purse and throw them out later? Since Rebecca had left without them, they couldn't have been anything she cared about. She'd made sure she had everything else from her purse, even though it'd all been on the bathroom floor like the papers.

I shoved them into my own purse. I'd dispose of them later.

Elijah looked in my direction and met my gaze. He held it.

"I hired her, Rebecca." His voice was firm and so calm it seemed almost inhuman. "She's here to deliver our weekly order of baked goods. The only one who doesn't have a legitimate reason to be here is you."

Rebecca's cheeks paled, making the arcs of her bronzer and blush stand out. "People aren't always what they seem."

She swept past me and took the stairs rather than the elevator, presumably so she didn't have to stand there and wait for it to arrive while we all watched her.

Everyone was still watching me anyway. A shiver slithered over my body, and I couldn't shake it out of my hands. They trembled against my legs. I stuffed them under my arm pits.

"Join me for a minute?" Elijah speared the three others with a look. "The rest of you have things you should be doing, do you not?"

The shaking in my hands spread up my arms. He'd sent Rebecca away, but that didn't mean he wasn't taking her accusations seriously. Considering Claire had grilled him at the tasting, he might have decided to cancel our contract.

Elijah closed the door to his office.

"I wasn't following her," I blurted. "And then she forgot her purse, and I was bringing it back to her when the door knocked it from my hands."

"You've very poor luck." Elijah leaned back on his desk and crossed his legs at the ankles. "But I asked you in here to apologize for Rebecca's behavior. She's always liked drama and to be the center of attention. We were all shocked when Uncle Donald married her. They were nothing alike. She likely would have left him long ago had it not been for the ironclad prenuptial agreement she had to sign before the wedding."

My brain kept circling around the knowledge that he hadn't brought me back to his office to fire me. He'd actually been embarrassed by Rebecca's behavior. The rest of what he'd said took a moment to sink in.

Rebecca had signed a prenuptial agreement. That meant that, had she divorced Donald or had Donald divorced her because of her affair, she likely would have gotten very little. It was the first hint that she might have had a motive for murder.

But only if she didn't know that she also wouldn't receive his fortune if he died before her.

Elijah had opened a door for me to find out. Unfortunately, it was a door I probably shouldn't walk through. If I asked any question right now, it might confirm Rebecca's accusations about me.

At the same time, if I didn't take this opportunity, Claire and I might as well give up on trying to help figure out who had killed Donald Wells. Dan would tell me that's exactly what we should do. But as long as Claire wanted to keep going with this investigation, I had to stick with her. She'd proven she couldn't do it on her own and also that she wasn't going to be able to rest until it was over.

I wasn't sure whether I would have walked away from the investigation or not had I been the only one involved. But I couldn't give up when Claire was still struggling. She'd given me a place to live, despite knowing that it might one day bring my crazy husband to her doorstep. She'd taken a risk on becoming my business partner, even though she knew Isabel Addington wasn't even my real name. The least I could do was investigate this murder if that's what it took to give her peace of mind again.

Besides, if Rebecca had killed her husband, I might have just made myself a target. She thought I was investigating her. Technically, prior to this moment, that hadn't been true. I'd been looking into her husband's death, but I hadn't considered her. Everything I saw pointed to her innocence.

I couldn't take that risk now. If I had to watch out for her, I needed to know.

My mouth felt so dry that my tongue could have been attached to the floor of it. I swallowed.

I had to approach this carefully, though. It couldn't sound nosy. Elijah would shut down the same way he had when Claire tried to pry information from him with a verbal crowbar.

It needed to sound like I was a little afraid of her. Like I needed him to rescue me again. Based on what I knew of him from his charitable giving and how he'd seen my reaction to Rebecca and wanted to reassure me, that was my best chance.

"I know this isn't my place, but she looked angry enough to kill when she left here, and I need to know if I'm in danger. If she could have murdered your uncle. She knew she wouldn't get anything in a divorce, but did she know she wouldn't get anything if he predeceased her?"

Elijah looked at me long enough that I was sure he wasn't going to answer. I wanted to squirm in my seat, but squirming was what guilty people did. I learned that early on when I needed to lie to Jarrod about something. Fidgeting indicated a guilty conscience, at least according to him.

I stayed as still as I could, shaking hands aside, and met Elijah's gaze.

He sighed in a way that sounded tired. "As much as I'd like to deny it, she did. My uncle had enemies who might have wanted to kill him, but I don't think my aunt—for all her flaws—was one of them."

13

For the first time in my life, bruises meant success.

Dan had been able to demonstrate how to escape a hold, and I'd gone through with it. I hadn't even felt discouraged when we'd passed the group class on our way out, and I saw how far ahead of me they were. I'd get there. I didn't have a timeline like they did. Dan said his friend ran this class every twelve weeks. We'd be able to keep coming as long as I needed.

Dan parked in front of Claire's house—my house—and gently pressed his fingers to his cheekbone. "Good thing you gave me this rather than the other way around."

I cast him a sidelong glance. "What? You wouldn't want to try to explain to people how you gave me a shiner?"

"I wouldn't want you to lose customers because you looked

like you got in a fist fight. If I go to investigate a case looking black and blue, suspects will think I'm tough."

He flexed a t-shirted arm.

Dan wasn't heavily muscled like the man who ran the self-defense class, but he was fit enough that flexing did show off his toned arm. The same arm that'd been around me more times than I could count now and was helping me learn to feel safe again.

There was a time when I thought that would never happen.

I laughed at Dan's joke and climbed out of the car.

"They're back," Janie's voice called out from the direction of the kitchen as soon as I opened the door.

She ran down the hall with Claire's *no running in the house* echoing after her. She stopped in front of me and thrust out a homemade card. The red construction paper sported a yellow flower, the two colors coming together to make the petals look distinctly orange.

I opened it. Inside, she'd printed her name in her big, blocky, just-learning-to-write style. She'd also drawn a heart.

Dan scooped her off the floor and planted a kiss on her forehead. "Where's my card, munchkin?"

He set her down, and Janie gave him her most serious face. "You've gotten plenty of cards from me. Isabel needed one."

My throat clogged. Which was stupid. A card shouldn't make me feel like crying. There wasn't even any reason to cry.

I blinked hard and gave Janie my biggest smile. "I'll put it on the fridge where I can see it every morning."

Janie nodded like she wouldn't have expected anything less.

Claire finally caught up to her and turned her around. "Go put away the crayons and the rest of the art supplies."

Janie glanced at Claire as if she was considering running there, but she skipped off instead. She cast a look back over her shoulder that clearly said *I'm not running*. Claire pretended not to notice.

She motioned Dan and me toward the living room. "I want to talk about the next steps for the business."

Dan hooked a thumb in the direction Janie had disappeared. "I'll get Janie and leave you to it."

"Oh no you don't." Claire clamped a hand around his wrist and practically dragged him to the nearest chair. "I want you to stay."

I dropped onto the couch and exchanged a quick glance with Dan. He shrugged. Claire hadn't warned him about this in advance.

We didn't exactly have next steps for the business. We weren't going to buy a second truck when we were still waiting on the insurance money from the first truck. Even if she was going to suggest that, I wouldn't go for it. Food trucks in Michigan were risky to begin with. Too many months of the year the area was devoid of tourists, and locals were too smart to stand out in the snow and ice to grab a cupcake.

Besides, even if Claire was going to argue that, she wouldn't need Dan to stay.

Dan leaned on the back of one of the chairs as if he didn't want to commit to sitting. "Not that I don't enjoy spending time with you both, but why do I need to be part of a business discussion?"

Claire sighed as if the answer should have been obvious. "Because she listens to you more than she listens to anyone else."

Was I the *she* in this discussion? Her words made me sound like a recalcitrant child. Or someone who couldn't take good advice.

And it also made it sound like Dan and I had some sort of different relationship than I had with her.

Dan and I were closer. But that's only because I wasn't sure half the time whether Claire actually liked me or not. It wasn't anything more than that. It couldn't be. Not with my situation.

Claire pointed at the chair Dan stood behind. "So sit."

At times like this, it was easy to forget that Claire was Dan's cousin, not his mother.

I considered crossing my arms over my chest the way Claire would have done had someone put her in a similar position. I didn't. What would have insulted me or at the very least made me defensive when I'd first met Claire I could now see as her way of handling stressful situations. She didn't seem to know any other way of getting what she wanted than to be pushy.

With most people, that approach would guarantee she wasn't heard. Most people would pull in the opposite direction the harder she pushed them. Or she'd steamroll over them, leaving enemies in her wake.

I wouldn't react in either of those ways. I wanted to prove her wrong that she needed Dan around for me to listen to her. Besides, I knew what it was like to not know how to get what you wanted. It wasn't always easy to ask. The mantra that *the worst that can happen is they say no* was entirely untrue. The *no* could come with embarrassment and mocking. The *no* could be an angry, dangerous no. Putting yourself out there, no matter how small the ask, wasn't easy. Sometimes bullying and demanding your way were a lot easier, even if people didn't like you afterward.

Claire stood in front of us, reminding me of someone making a presentation at a board meeting. "I want to make our partnership official and open a physical location, either instead of buying a new truck or alongside buying a new truck."

No way, was the first thought that jumped to my mind. "I can't put my name on any sort of contract or on a lease."

"You and I can write up an informal agreement, and I'll sign any legal paperwork. Having a partnership means you can have a permanent space."

Just like it means you can have a permanent home. Claire didn't say the words, but the implication was there. Because of

Claire's willingness to rent me a room without an official rental agreement, I could have a stable home. Claire declared the income and tithed on it, but she'd never asked me to put anything in writing that could come back to hurt me later.

Renting a space to run a shop was different, though.

"I know that face." Claire spread her feet slightly and planted her hands on her hips. "We need more oven space to keep up with our catering contracts now. And you know as well as I do that a food truck isn't going to give us both a livable income once winter hits. We need a stable location where people can find us, and where they can sit down with a cupcake and a cup of coffee."

I had to keep myself from glancing at Dan. If I did, it would only fuel Claire's belief that I would listen to what he suggested. Which wasn't entirely untrue. He was my friend and I trusted his opinion, so I did listen to him. But her suggestion that he could convince me to do something that I wouldn't otherwise do rankled. I'd promised myself that I wouldn't let another man control me the way Jarrod had.

What if Dan felt the same way Claire did? In the past, there'd been a couple of times when he'd asked me to do something odd and I'd done it. I turned to him unintentionally.

He held his hands up. "Nope. I'm not weighing in on this unless I'm explicitly asked."

All the weird fire that'd been building inside me since Claire's accusation died out. I should have known Dan wouldn't try to manipulate me into going along with Claire's idea, even if he agreed with her.

"If we had a retail location," Claire said as if Dan hadn't spoken, "we also wouldn't have to depend as much on big one-time events like the hot air balloon festival."

Her voice cracked slightly, and she stopped speaking.

I moved to the edge of my chair. Fear and I had been companions for so long that I recognized his fingerprint when I saw it. I knew her pushiness had to be covering up something she was much less comfortable facing.

She'd been trying everything she could think of to move past what had happened at the festival. Maybe she'd decided that the way to deal with it was to try to make sure she wasn't at an event where something similar could happen again. "Is that what this is really about? We won't be protected from death in a shop any more than we are in a truck."

"It's not about that."

The glare Claire gave me could have withered a flower, but the intensity of her reaction made me that much more sure I was right.

She huffed. "We didn't have a proper arrangement to do the tasting for Elijah Wells. We could get more jobs catering weddings and other formal events if we were able to offer a tasting menu in a shop." She dropped a sheaf of papers on the coffee table. "I've written up a tentative business plan and partnership agreement."

I could only imagine when she'd done that. If I had to guess, I'd have wagered it was when she should have been sleeping.

All of Claire's reasons for opening a permanent physical location were good ones. I agreed with all of them.

She'd missed the most important factor for me, next to not being able to put my name—real or fake—on a lease. "If I don't have a truck, I can't stay mobile."

The words sounded awkward coming out of my mouth, like I'd said something stupidly obvious like *if I don't have legs, I can't walk*. But surely they'd understand what I meant. Claire knew about Jarrod now. She hadn't asked me a lot of direct questions, but I'd shared a few more details since I'd come to live with her. Enough that she'd be prepared if he found me one day. Since I was living in her house, she needed to be prepared.

Dan leaned forward in his chair. I could feel his gaze on me. I looked up and met his eyes.

"You've decided to stop running," he said, his voice soft "Maybe it's time you also think about building."

Thinking about building meant thinking about a future. I hadn't been able to do that in a long time. Every step I'd taken since running from Jarrod had been focused on the present because that was all I knew I could have. A future was something else entirely.

Dan was still holding my gaze. Something in the way he was looking at me...it felt like there was more to what he was saying than the words.

Like he was talking about building more than my business.

I glanced down at the card from Janie. If I was going to build anywhere, this was where I'd want to do it. With him. With Janie. With Claire as my business partner.

The doorbell chimed.

Janie sprinted down the hallway from the direction of the kitchen. "I'll answer it!"

I couldn't hold back a smile even though she was disobeying Claire's *no running in the house rule* again. You'd have thought people at the door were bringing presents based on how much she enjoyed being the one to answer.

Janie's footsteps pattered back down the hallway and slowed right before they reached the door.

"There was no one there." She held up a rock. A small square of white paper the size of a business card was taped to it. Janie held it out to me. "I think this is your name."

I rose slowly from my chair and took the rock from her. My mind felt far away, as if it were floating high enough above the scene that nothing could touch it.

The piece of paper taped to the rock was a business card. Mine.

The inside of my head suddenly felt loud, like I was standing beside a semi-truck. Dan was saying something to Janie, but I couldn't make it out.

Why would someone have left a rock with my business card taped to it? It didn't make sense.

I pulled the card off and turned it over. Someone had scrawled a message on the back.

I know where you live.

14

*T*he rock slipped from my hand and hit the floor next to my foot.

"What are you doing?" Claire's voice was barely below a yell. "Do you want to break your toes?"

Dan had stopped his questioning of Janie. He rose to his feet.

I held the business card out into the space in front of me. I wasn't even sure who I was offering it to—Claire or Dan. I just didn't want to hold it anymore.

Claire snatched it from me. The muscles around the edges of her lips tightened. She shoved it into Dan's hand.

Janie bounced on her toes. "Was it a note? What does it say?"

Claire twirled her around until she faced back toward the kitchen. "Did you get everything cleaned up?"

Janie craned her neck toward the card now in Dan's hands. "Most of it. But then I got an idea for another picture."

Claire nudged her forward. "I'll help you finish while Daddy and Isabel talk."

"About the rock? Why would someone leave a rock with Isabel's name on it? I couldn't tell what it all said, but I saw her name."

Claire moved her out into the hallway. "Just someone playing a bad joke."

Their voices faded away. If only it could be just a bad joke.

"What if it's Jarrod?" My words came out sounding like someone was squeezing them. "There's no one else who'd do something like this. It has to be him."

Dan took my arm and eased me down onto the couch. I didn't even have the instinct to resist.

He sat beside me. "Is this Jarrod's style? From what you've told me, he sounds more like a man who'd grab you without warning. He didn't sound like someone who'd warn you he was nearby with a note."

My head nodded before I could consciously think it through. Jarrod wouldn't want to give me the chance to run or tell anyone. He was more likely to follow me down a dark street like the footsteps I'd heard the other night.

My phone and Dan's phone pinged with a text notification at the same time.

Dan glanced at his phone. "Claire sent a text to both of us. She heard your mention your husband's name. She wants to know if the handwriting looks like his."

I hadn't stopped to think about the handwriting.

Dan held it out for me. Unfortunately, we'd all touched it. The chances of gathering fingerprints from it, or the rock, were slim. Besides, most criminals nowadays were smart enough to wear gloves. We could thank crime shows for that.

I reined my thoughts back in and forced my gaze down to the card. The handwriting was loopy, almost ostentatious. It was so light in some places that the ink barely left a mark.

Jarrod's handwriting had almost been heavy and dark, and he almost never used cursive. He preferred to print.

I examined it for another few seconds to be sure.

My heart stopped pounding in my ears. I shook my head. "It's not his handwriting."

I pressed a palm to my forehead. My skin was clammy, but at least I could breathe again. "It's not him."

I'd never been able to move past a Jarrod scare this quickly and without Fear screaming at me to run before. Maybe what Dan had been saying before was right. Maybe it was time to build here, where I had people around me to see me through times like this.

Dan tucked the card carefully into his pocket.

His hand edged across the couch until his fingers rested gingerly on top of mine, as if he wasn't sure whether actually holding my hand would calm me down or freak me out more.

Maybe it should have scared me more, but all I could think about was that, whatever this was about, I wasn't alone.

I flipped my hand over and laced my fingers through his.

"Can you think of anyone else who might want to intimidate you?" Dan asked. His voice had an extra touch of gravel to it.

I couldn't stop myself from glancing toward the kitchen where Claire was distracting Janie. We'd agreed not to tell Dan that I was looking into Donald Wells' murder. Or, more accurately, Claire had told me not to tell Dan.

Technically, anyone could have gotten my card. I left a container of them on the counter of the food truck and I attached a card to any box of cupcakes I delivered. But multiple people connected to Donald Wells had my business card. Even Leon Schwab could have gotten one. All he had to do was take it off the box I delivered.

Avoiding Dan's disapproval suddenly seemed like the least of our problems. "You were right. About Claire and I getting involved in the Donald Wells case."

"Walk me through everything you did in the past few days."

He didn't remove his hand from mine the way I would have expected him too, but his voice was inflectionless. He'd put his detective's mask back on. My hand suddenly felt cold despite remaining nestled in his. We'd disappointed him.

Claire and I were both grown women. It shouldn't have mattered whether Dan was disappointed in us or not. But it did. At least to me. One thing my dad had taught me was that we all overestimated how smart we were. We were created to live in community, where we could surround ourselves with wise advisors, people who would help check us when we were about to do something stupid.

Perhaps that was the real reason neither Claire nor I wanted Dan to know what we were up to. Deep down, we both knew poking around in a murder investigation could turn out exactly the way it had—with a target on us.

I told Dan in detail about my last few days, especially delivering the cupcakes to Elijah, running into Rebecca, and overhearing her conversation with her boyfriend. I even included that I suspected someone had been hounding her for information prior to her husband's death.

Dan had pulled a notebook from his pocket and was writing notes throughout it all. When I finished, he slid it away again. "It sounds like something you stumbled on triggered the real murderer. Or, at the very least, made someone with something to hide nervous." He squeezed my hand. "But I'm even more sure now that this isn't Jarrod."

I nodded. We had so much at stake, whether Dan was right about that or not. And on both ends, the most precious thing was Janie. If this was Jarrod, and he got someone to write that note for him, I wouldn't let him hurt another child. I hadn't been able to protect our unborn baby from him, but he'd have to kill me before I let him hurt Janie.

If it wasn't Jarrod, Janie could still be in danger. Whoever sent the note wasn't subtle about knowing this was my home. They might also think Janie was my daughter. They might try to use her as leverage against me.

Dan didn't say anything about it, but I could tell from how close he kept Janie as they left that he'd thought about it too.

I WOKE UP TO THE VACUUM AGAIN SHORTLY AFTER TWO IN THE morning.

This had to stop. At the rate Claire was going, whoever sent that note wouldn't need to hurt us. We'd end up in the hospital from fatigue before they ever got to us.

I padded down the stairs. Claire had her back to me, methodically moving the vacuum back and forth across the already immaculate carpet.

I pulled the plug out of the wall. The room fell blessedly still.

Claire turned around with an expression on her face like she expected to find that she'd pulled the plug out of the wall accidentally. She wasn't wearing any make-up, and the bags under her eyes were so dark she almost looked like she'd been punched.

I braced myself for an angry outburst.

Instead, Claire stared at me. Tears slipped out of her eyes and sped silently down her cheeks. Not just a few either. Enough that they pooled and dripped down off her cheeks and I could see them falling to the floor.

"I don't know what to do." Her voice was hoarse. "I can't stop seeing it. Can't stop thinking about it. And now I'm thinking about the person who did that coming for us."

I nodded and took a step forward, then another. I didn't want to move too fast and risk that she'd shut down again and insist everything was fine. Everything—clearly—wasn't fine.

"I think it's time to go to a therapist."

Claire crossed her arms, and her body language started to change. It was so subtle that I would have missed it had I not spent so many years reading Jarrod.

I held up a placating hand. "Going to a therapist doesn't mean you're weak. It means you're strong enough to admit you need help."

It was something my friend Nicole had told me when she was trying to convince me to stay in her town rather than going on the run again. She'd even offered to pay for me to see a therapist. I hadn't been brave enough to accept her offer at the time.

Claire's arms loosened. And then she threw herself at me, hugging me so tight I could barely breath. Her tears soaked through my pajama top, leaving a wet patch.

For much too long I just stood there. It must have been like hugging a post. But she'd caught me off guard. I wasn't used to being dive-bomb hugged.

I eased my arms around her and patted her back. Maybe Claire was my friend after all. If she wasn't, she at least trusted me enough to show her soft underbelly. For a woman who was basically an armadillo, that was saying something. "I can go with you and sit in the waiting room if you want. No one has to know. Not even Dan."

This time, I felt entirely comfortable about leaving Dan out of the loop. As close as he and Claire were, and as much as he was the best friend I had, some things a person was still entitled to keep private. The need for counseling was one of them. Claire shouldn't have to tell anyone unless she chose to.

She nodded against my shoulder, then pulled away. She wiped under her eyes, even though she wasn't wearing any mascara to smear.

I pointed to the vacuum cord that I'd pulled out of the wall. "Do you want help cleaning?"

Claire shook her head. "One of us should get some sleep."

I wasn't likely to get much sleep now, but I appreciated the sentiment. I turned to go.

"Wait," Claire said. "Did you hang the car keys back up? If I stay here and clean, I'll keep you awake. My gym's open 24 hours. I might as well go there instead of vacuuming anymore. Nothing was coming up into the cylinder anyway."

Not surprising. If Claire vacuumed this stretch of carpet much more, there wouldn't be anything left of it. She'd probably vacuumed away half the fibers since Donald Wells' death.

I gave her what I hoped was a comforting smile. "They're still in my purse. I'll grab them for you."

Claire was particular about making sure everything in her house had a place and stayed there. Both of our purses hung right next to the door, on the same rack as the coats. Claire had once told me that was the best place to keep a purse because you were less likely to forget it and it was easy to grab in case of a fire. I'd lived in a food truck long enough before moving into her house that I hadn't even thought about needing to grab anything in a fire. I honestly didn't have anything worth saving in a fire.

I pulled my purse off the hook and fished around inside. The keys evaded me. Probably because of all the paper stuffed inside. Where had I gotten all this paper?

I scooped out a hand full. They were the bits and pieces that Rebecca Wells hadn't cared enough about to reclaim when they fell out of her purse. I'd forgotten all about them. It was past time to throw them out.

I collected the rest from my purse and found Claire's car keys at the very bottom, tangled up in the final receipt. I tugged them both out. The slip of paper had a name, phone number, and address on it. Rebecca Wells might actually miss this one once she went looking for it.

A sigh forced its way out. As much as I had other things I'd prefer to be doing right now—like sleeping—I should probably check the other pieces of paper in case they also had something written on them. When I made my next cupcake delivery to Elijah, I could leave them there for her to reclaim.

I smoothed the piece with the writing out on the counter. My hand froze. I knew that address. My friend Eve used to work at an insurance company located there. It was a street full of professional offices. Insurance, real estate…and lawyers.

Maybe the hot air balloon operator had been telling the truth all along.

15

*A*ndy Frank had claimed he'd asked Donald Wells to meet him at the hot air balloon festival because Andy saw Rebecca coming out of a lawyer's office. If Andy had been telling the truth about why he wanted to meet, it was highly unlikely he killed Donald.

Even though Donald hadn't believed Andy prior to climbing into the balloon with him, Andy's reason for meeting would be genuine. He hadn't lured Donald up there on false grounds intending to kill him.

"Did you find them?" Claire called from the living room.

I shoved the other papers back into my purse and tucked the one with the information into the pocket of my pajama pants. Claire was ready to get help. She didn't need something like this throwing her back into the investigation.

I wasn't even sure I should still be involved. But it wasn't like whoever sent the note didn't already know where I lived. They knew, and they knew Janie was here at least some of the time. The faster we figured out who killed Donald Wells, the faster Janie would be safe.

I put the car keys back in their regular spot. "They're on the hook. I'm headed to bed."

Claire made an affirmative noise. When I climbed the stairs and closed my own bedroom door, she was already up the stairs and back in her bedroom, probably changing into her workout clothes.

Before I did anything else, or told anyone else, I needed to confirm that the person Rebecca had written down was actually a lawyer. The address only proved where they were located. She might very well have written down the name and address of an insurance salesman or a chiropractor.

I turned the light off in my room and waited. Ten minutes later, Claire left her room.

I took out my phone and put the name into the search bar along with the word *Lakeshore*.

Kirkland Attorney at Law popped up as the first result. I clicked on the link.

The website looked professionally designed. Whoever put it together had spent the money and time to make sure it was mobile friendly.

I navigated to the Services page. Wills, trusts, powers of attorney, estates, real estate law, family law, and litigation.

Andy Frank probably *had* seen Rebecca coming out of Kirkland law office, but that didn't mean she'd been there for the reason he assumed.

Rebecca wouldn't have been going to a lawyer to file for divorce. She would have lost pretty much everything thanks to the prenuptial agreement she signed.

But maybe she'd been concerned enough about whoever she thought was following her to seek legal counsel. She might have been looking to file a harassment suit or something.

Rebecca had seemed pretty upset about the people who'd been bothering her prior to Donald's death. She also didn't seem like the kind of woman who would quietly endure that kind of treatment. Not if how she'd been acting since Donald's death was any indication.

The problem with my theory was she hadn't told Donald what she was doing, and she'd lied to the police.

I put my phone face down and laid back on my pillow. At this rate, Claire had a better chance of a full night's sleep than I did. There were too many questions rumbling around in my brain, and I couldn't do anything to follow up on them in the middle of the night.

I punched my pillow to fluff it up and turned over.

I could understand why Rebecca might have lied to the police, even after Donald's death. Whatever Donald had been up to, she didn't want the police to find out. If she admitted to going to the lawyer to deal with a quasi-stalker, she'd have had to give them the person's name. Then it wouldn't have been long before the police would have known everything. Donald's clandestine activities must have benefitted her somehow.

That explained why she'd gone to a lawyer instead of the police if someone was harassing her. She'd hoped the lawyer could handle it quietly.

But why lie to Donald about it? Had she been afraid he'd stop, and she'd lose the benefit of whatever he was into?

I flopped back to my other side, feeling a bit like a beached fish, floundering around.

Maybe I was making an assumption. Andy Frank assumed Donald didn't know Rebecca visited a lawyer. Andy assumed that because he thought Rebecca was trying to blindside Donald with a divorce.

Rebecca very well might have told Donald about her visit to the lawyer. Andy wouldn't have known that. And Donald either might have chosen not to tell him or he might have fallen out of the hot air balloon before he could.

All my theories hinged on why Rebecca went to the lawyer. If I could confirm it was about someone who was harassing her, then it would mean whatever Donald Wells had been involved in might very well have gotten him killed.

～

WHEN I WOKE UP A FEW HOURS LATER, MY EYES WERE GRITTY from lack of sleep. Claire must have come home sometime in the night without me hearing her because soft snores emanated from her room.

I'd never expected I'd be someone who could sleep that soundly. Not when Jarrod was still walking free in the world. Apparently, my middle of the night musings had exhausted my brain more than I'd realized.

I checked my cell phone. Eight-thirty in the morning. The lawyer's office might be open.

A text had also come in from Elijah. It'd probably been what woke me up.

Could you decorate a set of cupcakes with a tiny stethoscope, a band-aid, and pills that look like antibiotics?

A second text had come in a minute later.

We'll provide extra compensation of course. I'll call you later with the date and number we'd need.

I didn't do a lot of fancy decoration work anymore, but I used to enjoy it back when I'd been practicing because I thought I'd be going to culinary school. Polishing up my skills could only help out our business in the future.

Before I headed downstairs, I texted him back that I'd be happy to create what he was looking for.

I tiptoed down the stairs and out into the backyard. The air smelled like rain and the lavender Claire had in a pot next to the door.

I dialed the number.

"Kirkland Law Office," a bright female voice said. "How may I help you?"

"I just had some questions about your services. I read over everything on your website, but I didn't see if you ever did any harassment suits."

"Harassment is a criminal charge, so it's outside of our scope of practice. The most we can do is things like landlord-tenant and small claims court. You'd need a criminal attorney for that. I'd be happy to give you the name and number for a few that we've referred clients to in the past."

Thankfully, I didn't need that kind of service. That'd be quite the change in circumstance if I ended up charged with harassment. "I meant if I was being harassed and wanted to bring a suit against someone else."

"Oh, no." Her voice sounded genuinely regretful. "If you're being harassed, you'd need to go to the police, and they'll investigate it like any other crime."

So Rebecca hadn't gone to the lawyer for an official harassment suit. But possibly only because the lawyer couldn't do harassment suits? Obviously she wasn't going to take it to the police if she didn't want the police to know about it.

The non-criminal equivalent would be the restraining order she'd threatened me with. "What about restraining orders?

"We get requests sometimes, but you don't need a lawyer for those. At least not at the start. You might want a lawyer if the person you're filing against requests a hearing once he or she has been served. At the start, though, you just need to go to a courthouse and file." She lowered her voice. "Might as well save a little money."

If I'd actually been calling out of need, I would have appreciated her kindness. Her boss probably wouldn't like her telling potential clients that they didn't need his services.

"Sweetie, if you're in trouble, go right away. Don't assume you're making too much out of nothing, okay? As women, we're taught not to cause trouble or rock the boat, but sometimes the boat needs rocking. Especially if there's someone in it who should be tossed overboard."

My throat clogged. It was the kind of caring advice I could have used all those years that I talked myself into and then out of leaving Jarrod.

I'd been so isolated when I met him, and then he'd cut off my contact with the few friends I still had. I hadn't had anyone to give me that kind of nudge when the time came. I certainly wouldn't have been brave enough to call a lawyer. Jarrod checked all our phone records and grilled me about any number he didn't recognize. Once he'd actually called and screamed at a wrong number, threatening him with an arrest if he ever tried to contact me again.

"Thank you," I said. The word squeaked out in a voice so tiny it could have belonged to a child.

"My pleasure, sweetie. You call back if you end up needing

someone to stand beside you in court. I'll make sure Kirkland takes your case for half his normal fee. A wife's prerogative, you know."

I could practically see her wink at me. That also explained why she felt so free to say the things she said. If I ever needed a lawyer for something non-criminal, she'd made sure I'd hire them. Assuming I could afford them even at a discount.

We disconnected the call.

Based on what Andy Frank had said, Rebecca had gone to a lawyer for some reason. Whether it was this lawyer or another one didn't really matter. The most likely reason for visiting a lawyer seemed to be that she'd wanted to find a way to deal with the person or people who'd been hassling her.

Rebecca didn't seem like the kind of woman who would want to file for a restraining order herself. She wouldn't have cared about saving the money. At the time, she'd had plenty of Donald's money to spend, and she probably would have wanted to simply hire a lawyer to take care of it for her.

If the situation had gotten bad enough that she'd taken that step, then it also seemed likely this might have had something to do with Donald's death. Especially since she still wasn't willing to take the money in exchange for an interview even now that she didn't have Donald's wealth to live off of. That suggested that what he'd been doing was bad enough she didn't want to be connected to the scandal.

I needed to find out what was so condemning that Rebecca would keep it to herself even after Donald had gone to his grave.

In the bathroom, she'd mentioned that the Michigan Daily had offered her a significant sum of money if she would do an interview with them. Whatever reporter had contacted her clearly knew something the police didn't. Sometimes a reporter could give more focus to a story than a detective could to any single case. They could also pay sources and convince seedier people to talk to them.

And they wouldn't go to the police with what they knew. They wanted to be the one to break the story. They wouldn't risk a police gag order.

They also wouldn't tell me just because I asked. A reporter didn't uncover a story like this had the potential to be by being naïve or stupid. I'd have to convince them that I wasn't looking for information—I already had it.

I did a quick internet search and dialed the number that came up for the Michigan Daily. It was an area code I didn't recognize, so their office was probably located in one of the bigger cities, maybe even Detroit. The newspaper unfortunately hadn't listed numbers for individual reporters. If it had, I might have been able to compare the names with the types of stories they normally wrote and make a reasonable guess for the one most likely to be involved with a story about Donald Wells.

An automated system answered the call, directing me to dial

the extension of the party I was trying to reach or hit 9 to speak to the front desk. I hit 9.

"Michigan Daily," a woman's voice said. "How may I direct your call?"

I propped myself up against my pillows. "Who would I speak to about a tip for a story?"

"You mean a story idea that you want to write or you have information about an event that you think is newsworthy?"

The woman sounded bored, as if even a confession that I was a serial killer looking to do an exclusive with them wouldn't have merited her interest.

"Information about an event," I said.

"One moment please."

Before I could stop her and ask her who she was connecting me to, soft music filled my ear. At least I could be sure she'd placed me on hold rather than hanging up on me.

"Jackson Hogle." The man's voice was so loud and sudden that I almost dropped my phone.

He chose not to include a title of course. All I could do was stick to my plan and hope he knew enough about what was happening at the newspaper to know the name of the right reporter. The story couldn't be a complete secret. Someone had approved a large sum offer for Rebecca.

"I'm trying to reach the reporter who is writing a story on Donald Wells." I tried to keep my speech pattern slow and formal, mimicking Elijah's way of speaking as closely as I could.

If anyone at the newspaper had spoken to a family member, sounding like them might be enough to take down their guard. My imitation wasn't perfect, but hopefully it was enough. "I have information he wants."

"Okay," Hogle said, "tell me what it is, and I'll pass it along to her. If she thinks it's going to be useful, she'll get back to you."

Shoot. Bad assumption. Hogle now knew that I'd never spoken to the reporter writing the story. I should have chosen a gender neutral, but that would have required a really awkward sentence construction. He'd have caught on through that too.

Either way, I couldn't let him put me off. I could still handle this. "Mmm, I don't think so. I was told there would be compensation for what I know."

I sounded close enough to a combination of Elijah and Rebecca that if anyone had spoken to someone in the family I should bear a passing resemblance.

"Look lady, for all I know, you're from another paper fishing around for information. Or you're someone trying to stop this story, and as soon as you find out what reporter we have assigned to it, she *or he*"—he emphasized the pronouns as if to let me know that he might have been testing me earlier—"might disappear. You want to talk to anyone here, you can leave a name and number. We'll make sure you are who you say you are, and then we'll get back to you."

If I'd been one of his reporters, I would have been grateful for his protection. But really. Did I sound like I was a part of some gang or crime syndicate?

Then again, who knew. Donald Wells had been killed for some reason, after all. Maybe he was secretly a crime lord.

Now I sounded paranoid even for me.

Still, I couldn't leave my real name and phone number. They'd check me out and learn I wasn't connected to Donald Wells at all. Or, worse, they'd find out Isabel Addington didn't exist, and I'd end up as their next exposé. No, thank you.

I hung up.

I needed a new plan. The Michigan Daily definitely had a story brewing. They didn't seem able to go forward with it at present, but they were also protective of it. They weren't obligated to tell the police about it, and a lot of reporters took it as a note of pride that they wouldn't reveal their sources no matter what. Even threats of obstruction wouldn't make them budge.

Perhaps, though, a reporter would do a favor for another reporter? Assuming I could convince the only reporter I knew to help me. Again.

16

_T_he next day, I took the cupcakes I'd set aside from the batches I'd prepared to sell to my lunch crowd and headed for the building that housed the Lakeshore Daily. I didn't have to check the building directory, even though I'd only visited the offices once. The memory was seared into my mind.

They hadn't updated the clear glass door with the letters embossed on it. Inside, the set-up could have been pulled frozen from a time capsule. Same metal desks. Same extra wide aisles for Alan Brooksbank's wheelchair.

Alan would probably be able to work at the Lakeshore Daily for as long as he wanted to. His Positivity Project column had been growing in popularity. I'd even seen it mentioned online and heard it talked about on the radio. People enjoyed reading something that they knew would have a happy ending. It was why I read it. His column helped me remember that there was good in the world and good people.

I glanced around the room and spotted Alan's shaved head and bulky shoulders next to his desk. If it were possible, his muscles strained his black t-shirt even more than they had the last time I'd seen him a few months ago. The man really should participate in some sort of wheelchair sport with arms like that.

My stomach suddenly felt full of rocks. This was stupid. Alan Brooksbank had no reason to help me, and my cupcakes were nothing more than an obvious bribe.

But I didn't have any other option if I wanted to find out what Donald Wells had been doing that might have gotten him killed and now me threatened. And, more importantly, by extension, was a threat to Janie.

I crept forward until I was standing next to his desk. "Alan?" The word came out high-pitched.

He looked up with his double-wide smile on his face even though he couldn't have possibly recognized my voice—and wouldn't have had a reason to smile if he had. He was just that kind of nice person who smiled naturally.

His gaze hit my face, and his eyebrows rose slightly. "Isabel." The surprise in his voice was palatable. "I never thought I'd see you again."

"The feeling was mutual."

The words slipped out before I could stop them, another sign of how overly comfortable I'd become in my new world. I couldn't talk that way to men who weren't Dan.

Before I could cringe or apologize, Alan threw back his head and laughed.

"What brings you here? Did you sideswipe another vehicle?"

The way he said it and looked at me sidelong made me certain he knew I hadn't actually sideswiped any vehicle. Back when we'd first met, I'd used that ploy to convince him to get me information on Dan and Claire's cousin Blake. I'd suspected Blake of killing their grandfather. He hadn't. In fact, Blake turned out to be one of the nicest people, and he doted on his wife and children.

I set the box down on his desk. "I brought you cupcakes. Two of every flavor we made today."

Alan opened the box. The muscles on his arms bulged as he did. Could you eat cupcakes and have arms like that?

"Thank you." He took out one of the cherries jubilee. "I'll take the rest home. You just made two little boys very happy."

I hadn't thought about Alan having a family. I glanced at the hand holding the cupcake. Sure enough, he wore a simple gold band. It might have been there when we met the first time, but I couldn't remember.

A fleeting thought went through my head that Alan's wife was a lucky woman.

He was watching me with an expression that said he was still waiting for the real reason I'd come.

Without his help, I was at a dead end. Whoever left that rock would know where I lived, and there'd be nothing I could do about it.

I already knew Alan craved stories that ended well. Now I knew he was a family man too.

"The article you wrote about me and the little girl who I saved from the allergic reaction. She's part of my family now. I need your help to keep her safe again."

I gave him only the details he needed to know to want to help me. I didn't tell him I was trying to solve Donald Wells' murder. What I told him was that someone seemed to think I knew something about his murder, and they'd threatened us. I wanted to know who might have had a reason to kill Donald Wells so that I could pass those names along to the police. At the very least, I needed to know what Wells had been up to so the police could resolve this before whoever was behind it decided to hurt Janie.

The story was true. It was just abbreviated. Once I had the names, or even possible motives, I *was* going to hand them over to Dan.

Alan laced his hands behind his head and leaned back slightly in his chair. I felt as if I needed to stay still the way I would have had I been undergoing a medical scan. Instead of looking for a tumor or a lesion, he was looking for lies.

He sat up again and took a bite from his cupcake. "What, exactly, were you hoping I'd do?"

17

*I*t'd been a long time since I felt so in-control around a man. Not dominant. But as if I didn't have to be limp and allow things to happen to me.

Dan grabbed our water bottles from the side of the gym and handed mine to me. "That should cover any way someone tries to grab you, but we need to move to what happens if he manages to take you to the ground."

My brain felt like it collapsed into a small ball. It curled around my sense of self to protect it the way I used to curl up to protect my internal organs. I knew what happened when a man took me to the ground. Choking, punching, and other things I didn't want to remember.

My phone rang from where I'd left it on the bench next to Dan's gym bag. "I need a minute to even get my mind calm enough to try this. Let me get that."

Dan nodded.

I scooped up my phone. Elijah's number glowed on the screen. I slid my finger along the bottom to answer.

Elijah rarely jumped straight to the point. It was almost as if he felt it would be impolite. Each time he called me, he asked about my day and what I was doing. Taking so much time to talk to me wasn't efficient, but he seemed to actually want to know.

"I took your advice about the animals," he finally said once I finished talking about the women's self-defense lessons I was taking. I didn't have the courage to tell someone I'd met so recently that my sessions were one-on-one with a friend because I couldn't handle the pace or the male instructor in the regular class.

"What animals?"

"We're partnering with the local humane society. Once I learned more about the situation and how many healthy animals are euthanized each year, I knew it was a project we should be a part of. We're sponsoring a voucher system to allow people to spay and neuter for a minimal cost, and we're also looking at helping them build a bigger building."

A smile climbed over my lips. I hadn't expected him to actually look into it. "That's great."

"So I need you to start thinking about cupcakes that look like dogs and cats."

What had started as a simple "provide cupcakes for client meetings" had turned into something much more upscale. I'd been improving my techniques with fondant, gum paste, and modeling chocolate for weeks because Elijah kept calling and texting with special requests. The last one had been for a cupcake decorated to look like a beehive with a tiny bee on it. They needed something to donate for the silent auction the Save the Bees foundation was hosting.

Dan motioned to me that we should start up again. The main class would be winding down soon, and then we'd need to leave the gym.

"Do you have any specific colors or breeds of dogs and cats that you'd like me to model the design after?" I asked.

Elijah made a thoughtful *mmm* noise. "Allow me to get back to you on that."

We disconnected the call, and I rejoined Dan in the center of the mat.

"A good call?" Dan asked.

I realized I was still smiling. The thought of all those animals who'd be helped...it made me feel the way I'd felt when Janie picked out her cat from the shelter for her birthday. She'd walked past all the cute kittens and straight to an older cat with one ear. She'd named him *Pirate* even though it was his ear that was missing, not his eye.

"A good call. One of my new clients." I couldn't have explained why it felt so important to make sure Dan knew it was a business call. But it did. "He took a suggestion I made."

That tiny shift in expression that I couldn't explain crossed Dan's face and was gone.

"Let's set up for the next series of moves." He kept enough distance from me not to invade my space. Yet. "A large part of this for you is going to be a mental battle."

Dan knew my struggles well enough after all the time we'd spent practicing together. Each time we moved onto something new, we first had to desensitize me enough that I could even focus on what he wanted to teach me. My brain tended to short circuit even though I knew it was Dan and I knew it was safe. As soon as I was restrained, it didn't feel safe anymore.

He stepped closer. "Before we move to the floor, I want you to tell me how close I can get before you feel uncomfortable. Let's see what progress we've made."

I braced my legs slightly. "Okay."

He slid his hand into mine. His palm was rough and warm. "Is this okay?"

That had been okay for months. Not that we regularly held hands. We were just friends after all. But he took my hand enough that it felt normal. Comfortable.

I nodded in mock seriousness. "Unless your palms get really sweaty, that's fine."

Dan chuckled. "I'll keep that in mind." He stepped closer. Less than a foot separated us now. "And this?"

I waited for my body to tense, but it didn't. My mind felt

clear. Clear enough that I could notice how he smelled like coffee and soap. The smell was warm and clean and comforting.

But we'd been this close a handful of times too, even before training.

I looked up at him and smiled. "Still good."

Dan slid an arm around my waist and brought me in close. My hands instinctively rested on his arms just below his shoulders. He wrapped his other arm around my waist as well. His touch was gentle yet firm.

My stomach flipped, and my heart felt like it was pounding hard enough that he could feel it through my clothes. But not from fear. I struggled to make my mind remember where we were and that he was only holding me this close as an exercise and not for any other reason. Not because he wanted to.

Dan's eyes looked dark, and his gaze dipped to my lips. "And this?"

His voice was low. Tingles ran over my skin.

He was close enough now that if he lowered his head or I lifted mine up, our lips would touch. And for the first time in a long time, I wanted to be kissed. I felt safe here. I felt cared for here.

I felt wanted here.

Like I was someone special, not a constant disappointment.

He watched my face, waiting for an answer. The one I wanted to give him didn't involve words. I leaned forward.

My phone dinged with the special text message alert I'd set up for Alan so I'd know when he got back to me.

The sound was like popping a bubble. What was I thinking? What had I been about to do?

I stepped back, and he let me go. "I need to check that." My voice cracked on the way out. "It could be important."

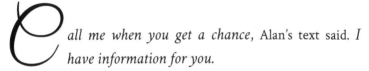

all me when you get a chance, Alan's text said. *I have information for you.*

I glanced over my shoulder at where Dan packed up his gym bag, looking as if we hadn't nearly kissed. Maybe we hadn't. Maybe that had been all in my head. It wasn't like I routinely got that close to men. In fact, I tried to avoid getting close to men.

Maybe I was just projecting. Dan had been a good friend to me. My best friend. My first best friend since childhood. Emotions couldn't always be reasoned with, and mine had probably gotten friendship confused with more. My body no longer reacted to him with fear. Surely the desire to kiss him was a confused echo of that.

More importantly, I was a married woman. I couldn't indulge those feelings, whether or not they were real or reciprocated. Not with Dan. Not with anyone.

I had to act like nothing had happened.

Besides, he probably wouldn't want to kiss me anymore—assuming he had in the first place—once he learned about me contacting Alan.

But I had to tell him. If Alan had information that could point to who had killed Donald Wells and left me the threatening note, Dan needed to know.

I turned back to face him. "I did something you're not going to like."

Dan slowly zipped up his duffle bag and straightened. "Okay?"

He really must have made a great undercover police officer. His expression gave absolutely nothing away. I couldn't tell if he was worried, annoyed, or still thinking about that almost kiss.

I explained what I'd done and why I'd done it. "I don't know what he found out yet, but I wanted to have you on the phone call with me when we find out. I'm not trying to investigate this alone or hide anything from you."

An expression flickered across his face that I couldn't interpret, there and gone so fast that the only tell was its existence at all.

I played my own words back in my mind. I probably sounded like a liar to him. I *had* tried to investigate on my own by calling the lawyer and trying to contact the reporter. But I'd done it with the intention of turning anything I learned over to him, not with the intention of continuing to look into it myself. "Any more than I already have, I mean."

A smile played at the corners of Dan's lips, and the smile crinkles that always made my stomach feel warm formed at the corners of his eyes. "I was thinking that you do a cute thing where you bite the edge of your lip when you're nervous, but that's good to know."

I threw a mock scowl at him. "Do you want to listen to the phone call or not?"

Dan motioned me over to a bench along the wall and patted the spot beside him.

I dialed Alan's number.

"That was fast," he said instead of hello. "I just texted."

He must have attached my name to my number in his phone. It left a weird feeling on my skin, like wearing new clothes that I wasn't entirely comfortable in yet. I now had people who expected to hear from me often enough, who expected to know me long enough, that I was a contact in their phone.

"I have you on speakerphone with a friend of mine who's also one of the detectives working the case. Detective Holmes. You've met before. More than once."

"I remember. Nice to talk to you again, Detective." Dead air filled Alan's end as if he were considering something. "The story's dead anyway, so I think he'll be okay with this going beyond Isabel."

The other reporter was a *he* after all. Jackson Hogle at the Michigan Daily *had* been trying to play me.

"Do you need to confirm with him?" Dan asked. "If this sounds like a genuine lead in the murder investigation, I'll need his name and contact info, so I can follow up with what he knows."

"I'm sure." No hesitation on Alan's part now. "He's one of the good guys. He writes a different type of story from me, but he tries to expose corruption, not just write whatever will sell the most papers for a day."

Dan made an approving noise that made me think he'd run into too many reporters who would spin a story for exactly the purpose of selling more papers, whether the story was entirely accurate and well-researched or not. Nowadays, most reporters wrote in order to further an agenda rather than objectively presenting facts even.

"That's actually the only reason he was willing to talk to me," Alan said. "He knows I wouldn't try to write the story half-baked. It's not my type of story."

Alan's column was the only thing I read in the newspaper for that very reason. His stories left me feeling like there might still be hope in the world, good in the world. Everything else in the news made me either afraid to go out my door or feeling like the world was going to pieces around me and there wasn't anything I could do about it.

"So he told you everything he'd collected for his story?" I

asked.

"He did."

Alan's end of the line was too quiet for the newsroom. I couldn't help but wonder where he was, but I wasn't surprised he'd left the main room of the Lakeshore Daily. Many of his coworkers might respect the situation. Most of them were probably ethical and wouldn't try to scoop the story. But all it took was one person to overhear and run with it.

"He got an inside tip from someone close to Donald Wells who said Wells was embezzling from the family business and their clients. If it continued much longer, the damage to the business was going to be irreparable. And not only in reputation."

Irreparable damage to the business gave a lot of people motive if they'd found out. Everyone who worked there in fact.

Including Elijah, my brain hissed at me.

I wasn't stupid. I knew Elijah might have a motive already. I still didn't believe he would have killed his uncle over it. Reported him to the authorities for sure, but murder?

Reporting him could have destroyed the business, the annoyingly logical side of my brain said.

I told it to shut up. It was better than Fear, but that didn't mean I had to listen to everything it said.

Elijah wasn't the only one with a business-based motive. Rebecca's boyfriend would have had a motive too. Not only would killing Donald have freed up Rebecca to marry him—or so he clearly believed—but it might have also saved his job and allowed him to move up in the company.

"Did he dig up anything else?" Dan asked, effectively putting an end to my brain spinning its wheels.

"Not much. He tried to investigate further. He even followed around Wells and his wife for weeks hoping to catch a lead. Finally, he offered the wife a huge sum of money if she'd confirm what the other source said and answer some of his questions. She refused and threatened him with a restraining order."

At least I knew my theory about Rebecca was partially right. She must have figured out that the reporter was following her. She wouldn't have known at first who he was or what he wanted. Once she knew his name, she might have wanted to take precautions to make sure he legally had to leave her alone.

"The reporter I know couldn't prove anything," Alan said, "so he eventually had to drop the story."

"Will he share the information he was able to gather with me?" Dan asked.

"I'll have him get in touch."

I ended the call.

Dan squeezed my hand, quick and then gone. "The department can subpoena records that Alan's friend couldn't get. Once we know who would have known about what Donald was doing, we'll be able to make some arrests, either for embezzlement of accomplices or murder. I think this is almost over."

19

When you bring the cupcakes up today, Elijah's text message said, *leave them at Mary Ellen's desk. I'll be waiting in my office.*

I leaned my head back against the headrest, my chest feeling like I'd been hit with a deployed airbag. That message definitely sounded like he was about to fire us. Maybe I should turn the truck around and not go in at all.

I'd thought everything was going well. I'd met all of his unique requests. I'd made sure to come without Claire. We'd chat for fifteen or twenty minutes every time I dropped off the weekly cupcake order. He'd even text me sometimes during the week to tell me about the current charity they were working with.

But just because he seemed to like me as a person didn't mean he'd necessarily want to keep working with us. He might have even found out that I'd been snooping around in his uncle's death and trying to prove that one of his employees was behind it. Elijah didn't seem like the kind of man who'd stand for that.

I sucked in air, and the tight feeling in my chest eased slightly. Losing this contract wouldn't be great for business, especially with Claire still pushing the idea of us setting up a physical location. But it wouldn't destroy us.

Box of cupcakes in my arms, I headed into the building. The security guard knew me so well that I didn't even have to stop. He passed me through with a smile and a wave.

Mary Ellen sat behind her desk when I reached their floor. She looked like she'd been perching on the edge of her seat, watching for me.

"Go right in," she said. "He's waiting for you."

My throat felt suddenly dry. Mary Ellen didn't seem upset. She seemed almost...excited. That couldn't be right if she knew Elijah planned to fire us. She liked my cupcakes.

I set the box of cupcakes down. "There's an extra in there for you. Strawberry shortcake this week."

She peeked towards Elijah's office door and slid the box toward her. "You're an angel, you know that."

I forced a smile that I didn't feel and headed for Elijah's office. Even if he fired us, we'd still get work simply from having this contract. Mary Ellen had even been talking to me about catering her sister's bridal shower.

This was going to be okay. It was.

I opened Elijah's office door, and a black dog that looked like a six-month-old Lab bounded up to me. He wriggled and licked my hand and wriggled some more as I tried to pet him.

Three more dogs followed on his heels—one with long floppy ears, another with a super fluffy brown coat, and a third that was all angles and looked like she hadn't grown into her feet.

"I wish I had four hands right now, so I could pet them all."

Elijah laughed his soft chuckle. I hadn't realized I'd spoken that out loud until his reaction.

I glanced up at him. His tie was slightly askew, and he had a smear of what looked like dog slobber up his pant leg.

"The people from the shelter will be back to collect them in approximately half an hour," he said. "But I wanted them to bring the dogs here so you could base your cupcake designs on them. The cats are next door in the conference room. We'll go there next."

What he was saying couldn't have made less sense if he'd been speaking Italian. "My cupcake designs?"

I parroted his words back at him even though I knew it made me sound stupid. I couldn't think straight with so many adorable dogs vying for my attention anyway. They wanted my attention even more than my friend Nicole's dogs had, and that was saying something.

"Apparently our social media feed jumped in whatever metrics those types of sites use when we shared we were raising funds for the shelter. The rest of the board and I decided to increase our partnership and host an adoption event. We want it to be a big enough event that it merits news coverage to increase awareness. I'd like you and your partner to cater the event."

I sagged back against the door and then had to brace myself against the wall as the dogs sensed my moment of weakness and swarmed me. That was the opposite of getting fired. An event like this would also bring press to How Sweet It Is. And thanks to my partnership with Claire, she could be the face of the business while I stayed out of a photographers' range.

A knock sounded on the door behind me.

"Mr. Wells?" Mary Ellen's voice was higher than usual and had a wobble to it. "There are some people here to see you."

Elijah's eyebrows drew down in the center, as if he couldn't understand who could have gotten up here without an appointment. Who would dare? Who that Mary Ellen wouldn't simply send away or call security on if they refused to leave?

The police. It hit me at the same time as it must have occurred to Elijah because he glanced at me and then at the door.

"Show them in."

Dan entered with two uniformed officers. His gaze landed on me, and the lines around his lips tightened almost imperceptibly. I only recognized it because I knew him so well.

He hadn't thought I'd be here. Maybe he didn't even realize Claire and I had accepted a contract with the business. I couldn't remember if either of us had actually told him.

My throat felt like a rope had coiled around it. If we hadn't thought to specifically tell him that our new contract was with the Wells' family business, it would look like I'd intentionally hid this from him. Like I'd lied to him after saying I didn't want to lie to him.

"Elijah Wells," Dan said without looking at me again, "you're under arrest for the murder of Donald Wells."

The older of the uniformed officers stepped forward and recited the Miranda warning.

One of the dogs licked my hand, and I stroked his soft head. This couldn't be happening. It was all wrong. They'd gone to the wrong office and gotten the wrong name. The trail was supposed to lead to Leon Schwab.

Elijah left the room with them without resisting or saying anything other than instructing Mary Ellen to watch the dogs until the people from the shelter returned.

Dan turned toward the door as well. I grabbed his sleeve.

He turned back to me and raised his eyebrows.

The look in his eyes was angry, but there was also something else. Something that looked so much like disappointment that I almost couldn't breathe. He did think I'd lied to him.

My lips felt encased in cement. For the first time in a long time, my first instinct wasn't to run. It was to fight.

To fight for Elijah because I couldn't have been deceived about a man again. The first time I'd met a man other than Dan who I wasn't afraid of couldn't be the time that man turned out to actually be dangerous.

I'd spoken to him. We'd texted. He listened to me enough that they were supporting an animal shelter, for crying out loud. He wasn't a murderer. He couldn't be a murderer.

I couldn't have that little ability to tell a good man from a bad one. If I could be so wrong, what was to say I wasn't wrong about Dan too?

And if I was wrong about Dan...I couldn't even finish the thought.

The way he was looking at me now, maybe it wouldn't matter whether I'd been wrong about him or not. He might not want me in his life anymore.

I had to fight for him too. Especially for him. I'd rather lose my truck, my whole business, than lose Dan and Janie.

All the things I wanted to say jumbled up in my mind. I didn't even know where to start.

"Well?" Dan's tone was colder than he'd ever used with me before. "I can't stand here indefinitely. I have to get back to the station."

I took a step back.

Fear banged on the door in my mind where I'd locked him.

I swallowed hard, forcing my throat and lips to work again. "This is a contract. I'm here for a contract. Elijah hired Claire and I to provide cupcakes for their client meetings." I gestured at the dogs. "I'm supposed to design cupcakes based on these guys for their upcoming fundraiser."

Dan's face didn't soften. "Do you call all your clients by their first name?"

What did that have to do with anything? "We've gotten to know each other over the past few weeks." Heat bubbled in my stomach, and my hands tightened, wanting to make fists. Maybe it was lying to omit that Elijah had asked me to call him by his first name from the start, but Dan's words had felt a lot like an accusation. He seemed to think there was something unprofessional happening here. "But yes, I do call many of my clients by their first names. I make cupcakes. I'm covered in sugar and glitter half the day. It's not exactly a formal business."

A muscle twitched in Dan's cheek, almost as if his face wanted to smile, and he wouldn't allow it. "You might want to start being more selective about which clients you choose to befriend."

Ouch. And unfair. The last murder I'd been involved in investigating, the friend I'd made hadn't even done it. She'd been innocent. If I hadn't been her friend and hadn't been willing to fight for her, she might have wrongfully gone to prison.

The heat inside flared into flames. He didn't have any right to be angry with me. I hadn't done anything wrong.

"Elijah couldn't have done this. He's not that kind of person."

Dan's jawline hardened into stone. "Your lead brought us here. I traced the anonymous source to Elijah." He emphasized his name. "The whole team spent the past two weeks confirming it. We subpoenaed phone records. There's no doubt he tipped off Alan's friend at the Michigan Daily."

I couldn't accuse Dan of rushing into this. He was good at his job, and the phone call with Alan had been almost three weeks ago now. "Just because he's the anonymous source doesn't mean he killed his uncle."

"We've interviewed employees here who confirmed there seemed to be a break between Elijah and his uncle prior to Donald Wells' death. We believe Elijah tried to talk to his uncle first, and his uncle either denied any wrongdoing or refused to stop. That's when Elijah went to the reporter, thinking that if his uncle felt some pressure from an investigation, he'd stop what he was doing before it ruined them. When that failed too, he killed him."

The theory wasn't outlandish. Elijah cared deeply about this business and the good they could do through it. I'd learned that this small part of the building wasn't the whole business. It was only their charitable division. Elijah had turned down a more prestigious role in the company to head this division.

If anything would push him to murder, losing the ability to do good here would be it.

What if I *was* wrong about him?

My legs felt weaker than if I'd run a marathon. I rested a hand on the head of the black lab to brace myself.

I'd always been a horrible judge of character. Jarrod had proven that. He was supposed to be my knight in shining armor, my one true love, my everything promised by romantic comedies and sappy movies.

He'd turned out to be the opposite. Maybe everyone wasn't what they seemed. Not Jarrod. Not Elijah.

Not Dan.

That's what I've been trying to tell you, Fear's voice hissed in my head.

If Fear was right, then everything I'd come to care about—everyone I'd come to love—was lost.

I forced myself to look at Dan even though the way he was looking at me made my heart feel bruised. "How can you trust anyone in this world? You see this all the time." I couldn't miss the echo of Claire's earlier words in my mind. She'd wondered how Dan managed to see carnage and death on a regular basis without breaking. I understood that. A person could work through that. But emotional carnage—that I had no idea how to survive. "How can you ever have a relationship if people can lie and deceive and hurt each other?"

My words came out so soft I hoped he could hear them over the panting dogs and clicking nails on the floor.

Dan's hands twitched as if he wanted to run them over his face or rub the back of his neck, but his training wouldn't allow him to give in to that kind of a tell. "Were you thinking of having a relationship with him?"

I felt like I was in a carnival fun house where all the floors were uneven and the mirrors reflected back distorted versions of the world. We didn't seem to be having the same conversation.

I kept my gaze steady on his even though it felt like doing so might crack me open. That was probably one of the skills that made him such a good undercover officer in the past and such a good detective now. No one could lie to him when he looked at them like this.

"A friendship. I thought we were friends or could be friends. I don't have enough of those."

Dan stepped closer, halving the distance between us. "You have more than you think."

My mind flashed back to when I'd been sitting at his kitchen table, and he'd been trying to convince me to stay in Lakeshore where I had friends. At the time, it'd been only him and Janie, with his assurance that Claire would eventually come around.

He'd been right then. He was right now too if I stopped to count them. Nicole was my friend and was still there for me when I needed her, even though she lived in Fair Haven instead of in Lakeshore. I had Eve, who still showed up at my truck daily, only now every Wednesday she did it when the rush was over, and she brought a meal for us to share. Even Alan Brooksbank was my friend, in a weird way, if a friend was someone you could go to when you needed help, and they came through for you.

Very few people could count that many true friends in their lives. Having that many made me blessed.

I nodded.

Dan closed the rest of the gap between us. He cupped my face in one hand and ran his thumb gently along my cheek bone.

Tingles shot through every inch of my body.

"Why do you feel like you don't have enough?" His words were almost a whisper. "Is there something we can do to let you know you're already cared about?"

My pulse beat at the back of my throat.

Don't have enough.

My eyes stung. I hadn't had enough friends to protect me when my dad died and I got involved with Jarrod. There wasn't anyone to point out the red flag or tell me I was moving too fast. I hadn't had enough friends to stick around when he isolated me. I hadn't had anyone to fight for me when I needed it.

Was I still trying to fix that when I kept feeling like I didn't have friends and needed to cling to every chance for one?

Dan was still looking at me, his thumb stroking my skin, all the anger and disappointment and any other negative emotion I'd seen before gone.

Waiting for my answer.

"The more friends I have, the more likely at least one of them won't abandon me when I need them. If Jarrod..."

I couldn't finish the thought. Fear keened in my head when I tried until I felt like I might pass out if I had to say the words.

"I'm not going to abandon you." Dan's voice was soft yet firm.

He'd shown me that over and over again. And yet the way I'd felt when I saw that note on the back of the business card was still fresh. This wasn't just about Dan or me or our friendship. "Not even when someone threatens Janie, if Jarrod threatens Janie?"

"Not even then. We'll keep her safe together." His eyes darkened, and his gaze dropped to my lips. "You matter that much."

I shifted my gaze down, away from his. I hadn't imagined it the other day. He had wanted to kiss me. He wanted to do it now.

And I wanted him to.

But I still couldn't let him. We were playing on the edges of something that could destroy us both. I was a married woman. I'd come back to my faith in God in the last few months, and I couldn't do damage to that new faith and relationship with Jesus by willfully doing something I knew was wrong. No matter how much I wanted it.

Dan shared the same beliefs I did. As long as I was married, anything we did would be adultery.

"You know that friendships are all I can have."

The words felt like I was carving out my own heart with a spoon. This wasn't fair. Yes, I'd made my choice when I married Jarrod, but I hadn't gotten what I'd bargained for. I had grounds for divorce, but I couldn't even divorce him. Filling for divorce would give him my address and assure that he found me and killed me before I could ever expose in court everything he'd done.

This wasn't fair. I directed the thought heavenward this time.

"I'm still married," I choked the words out.

I couldn't see Dan's face. His lips pressed against my forehead, light and warm, and then he was gone.

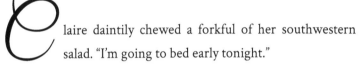laire daintily chewed a forkful of her southwestern salad. "I'm going to bed early tonight."

We'd recently decided to take turns cooking meals rather than continuing to eat separately. Whenever it was her turn to cook, it was some variation on salad. The child I'd once been missed cupcake leftovers for every meal, but the grown woman already felt how much more energy I'd had since my diet began regularly including fresh things.

"With Donald Wells' murderer in prison," she said, "I'm finally going to be able to sleep."

The human brain didn't always work that way. Sometimes, even after the danger was gone, a person could remain hyper-aware of everything around them. Claire might find there were still times when something triggered those memories, and she couldn't focus or couldn't sleep.

Besides, if she only felt safe because she thought the murderer was locked away, that restfulness would be short-lived. A man like Elijah was probably already out on bail. It'd only be a matter of time until Claire learned he was walking free until his trial.

But I hoped I was wrong. If Claire found peace from Elijah's arrest, that'd be one of us at least. Maybe I was in denial the way Dan had implied, but I still couldn't imagine Elijah killing his uncle.

I rolled a black bean around on my plate. "Dan told you Elijah Wells was arrested?"

Claire made an affirmative noise, her mouth full.

Dan hadn't contacted me since our conversation in Elijah's office that afternoon. I probably shouldn't have expected him to. I'd basically told him that we had no future. Whatever I felt for him, whatever he might feel for me, couldn't go anywhere as long as I was married.

We'd both known that from the start. I don't know how I'd let my emotions run out of control. Maybe I'd been so busy denying to myself that I felt more than friendship for Dan that I hadn't paid enough attention to what I actually felt. Maybe if I'd acknowledged it to myself, I could have smothered those feelings earlier, when they were weak and easy to kill.

And maybe tomorrow I'd wake up and the sky would be green and the grass would be blue.

Regardless of all of that, despite knowing Dan was making

the right choice in backing off, I missed him already. I missed our regular texts and the way he'd call at the end of the day to see how I was. I missed hearing his voice and the way it made me feel calm. And it'd only been a couple of days.

If we couldn't find a new normal in our friendship, I'd miss a lot more things in the coming days.

And I didn't know where this left Claire and me with Elijah's company. Was I still supposed to bring cupcakes? Would there still be a fundraiser to cater?

All selfish thoughts.

"Stop playing with your food like a five year old," Claire said.

I straightened in my chair and obediently shoveled a bite of food into my mouth.

Claire removed her empty plate from the table. A yawn split her jaw, and she covered it with her hand. "I'm going to take a long, hot bath and climb into bed early enough that I could be a five year old."

I put another bite of food into my mouth so that she didn't feel the need to stay and make sure I finished my dinner.

She rinsed her dinnerware and placed it all in the dishwasher.

Then I was alone with my thoughts.

It wasn't a place I enjoyed being right now. In the same way that Claire hadn't been able to stop thinking about Donald Wells plummeting to his death and his murderer walking free, I wasn't able to stop thinking about an innocent man potentially going to prison for it. That didn't benefit anyone. Convicting an innocent person didn't get justice for Donald Wells.

It also meant that all the good work Elijah had been doing for charities would stop, at least temporarily. Whoever took over for him might not have the same heart for it or the same skill with it.

Elijah didn't deserve to go to prison if he didn't do this.

That's his lawyer's job, Fear said in my brain. *You need to stay out of it now.*

I should have never let Fear back out of his box.

But he wasn't wrong. Elijah would hire a lawyer. That lawyer would defend him. That lawyer would also drain a lot of money, either from the family business if they voted to support him or from Elijah personally. Besides, as I'd learned from Nicole, my lawyer friend, most lawyers didn't care if their client was guilty or innocent. Some of them didn't even want to know.

Elijah needed a lawyer like Nicole. Lakeshore was a little far for her to travel in her current condition, but she might be willing to do it anyway.

But she wouldn't do it unless she was absolutely confident that Elijah was innocent. Nicole only defended innocent clients. That was one of the things I respected so much about her.

Before I asked her to come all this way to meet with Elijah and consider his case, I needed to be certain I was referring an innocent client to her.

I needed that reassurance too. Dan had been right that I had a lot of friends now, and I didn't need to feel like I was lacking. All those friendships depended on trust, though. I had to believe I could tell good people from bad and that I'd picked good people to be my friends. I had to know I wasn't so easily deceived. I'd been wrong about Jarrod, and that needed to have taught me something.

I forced down another bite of salad. All I had to do was figure out what that step should be.

The reporter who'd been investigating the case wouldn't give me any information, even if I asked. He'd already turned over everything he had to the police, and that led to Elijah anyway.

I couldn't get access to Elijah while he was in jail awaiting bail. Dan certainly wasn't going to share details of the case with me.

That left me one person who knew what Donald had been doing and who might know who else knew about it or had been in on it.

Rebecca Wells.

The trick would be convincing her to talk to me.

21

I took Claire's car since I knew she wouldn't need it to go to the gym for once and drove to Rebecca Wells' house. I couldn't risk calling first. She'd never agree to talk to me if I called and asked permission. I'd have a hard enough time convincing her to help me help Elijah as it was. Based on what I'd seen, there wasn't any love lost between them.

I parked behind the cars in the driveway. A pack and move container also sat near the garage. The estate must have been settled, and Rebecca was preparing to move. My timing was perfect. If she'd moved already, I wouldn't know where to find her, and I certainly couldn't ask Elijah.

Hopefully Rebecca would answer the door herself rather than someone else. I didn't know if she kept a housekeeper or a cook, but it seemed likely.

I rang the doorbell.

The door opened almost immediately. Rebecca stood in the doorway, one manicured hand resting on the door frame. A frown pursed her lips.

"Who is it?" a man's voice asked from inside.

I'd heard that voice before, but I couldn't pinpoint where. It wasn't Elijah's. I knew that much at least.

"It's the woman who's been following me."

I wanted to crinkle up my nose, but I forced myself not to. With an introduction like that, I wasn't likely to be able to win over whoever she was with to my side—assuming she was willing to talk in front of him.

"Invite her in," the man said.

Rebecca's lips pouted slightly. "We don't need to talk to her."

"We do if she's snooping around in your private affairs. We need to resolve this."

"Fine." Rebecca opened the door wider and stepped out of the way. "Come in."

I entered. The door snicked shut behind me, and a gun pointed at my face.

My mind went numb, and my vision blurred. I put my hands up automatically to show I wasn't armed and I wasn't a threat.

"I don't understand." The words came out almost without me willing them. "I'm not here to threaten her, I promise."

I drew a deep breath. My vision cleared slightly. Leon Schwab stood in front of me, holding the gun pointed at my heart now instead of my face. Rebecca moved around to stand beside him.

This didn't make sense. She'd broken up with him, hadn't she?

Leon poked the gun toward me. "Then why are you here?"

Honesty seemed like the best policy when faced with a deadly weapon. "I wanted to talk to her about her husband's death. About who might have wanted him out of the way. I don't think Elijah did it, which means whoever did is still loose." Rebecca didn't strike me as the altruistic sort. If I made this all about Elijah, she wasn't as likely to help me. It needed to also be about her. "If you tell me the truth, I can help you stay safe."

Rebecca's face went pale even under her make-up. "Was that a threat?"

What? How could she interpret that as a threat?

Leon's eyes narrowed slightly, as if he were trying to see through me. "Are you an undercover cop?"

"No. I'm not even comfortable around police."

"That's a lie," Rebecca whispered. Maybe she thought I couldn't hear her, but I was close enough she would have had to speak right into his ear if she didn't want me to know what she was saying. "She's living with a cop's relative, and he's always around."

A shiver ran over my skin as if someone had swapped out the blood in my veins for freezing rain. Rebecca knew who I lived with. If she researched our business after Claire and I showed up at the funeral luncheon, she would have been able to learn Claire's name. Claire's photo was on the website. A simple internet search would have turned up the rest. Claire was still listed in the online phone directories.

She could have learned all that about Claire from the internet, but she couldn't have known that I lived with Claire. Or that Dan was always at our house.

She could have only known that if she'd been following me. If she knew where I lived.

The handwriting on the card tied to the rock had been all loops. It could as easily have been a woman's writing as a man's. And I'd handed Rebecca one of my cards to prove who I was the day we met in the restroom.

If Rebecca had been the one to try to scare me away, she might also have been the one to kill Donald. Except that she didn't have a motive. It didn't make sense.

I edged backward toward the door, keeping my hands up. "If you let me leave, I won't come back, and I promise I won't seek Rebecca out again."

I prayed they'd hear the honesty in my words and not sense the deception underneath. I wouldn't need to seek Rebecca out again because I'd tell Dan about this, and he'd take over from there.

Rebecca and Leon exchanged a look.

"She might be a cop or a reporter," Leon said, "or just some busybody, but she knows too much if she came here to talk to you."

Rebecca nodded slowly, as if she knew he was right, but she didn't like the implications of what he was saying.

The words *she knows too much* never boded well for someone with a gun pointed at them.

"I don't actually know anything." I shifted another inch toward the door. It was closed, but it was my only hope. I'd never get my phone out and dial for help faster than Leon could pull a trigger. If I got outside, they'd be less likely to shoot me. One of the neighbors might see. "I thought Rebecca might know of someone else who might have wanted Donald dead because of his embezzling."

Leon's face hardened, all remaining soft edges gone. "If you figured out the embezzling, you already know too much."

Rebecca put a hand on his forearm, as if she didn't want him to do whatever he was considering. "I didn't take part in that. It doesn't matter what she knows."

"The police will take everything if they find out, and then it'll all have been for nothing."

My heart beat so hard that I could feel it at the bottom of my throat and in my temples. Rebecca enjoyed her lifestyle, but she hadn't been comfortable with the way her husband was supplementing it. That felt like it should be important, but I couldn't put the pieces together.

Possibly she killed him to stop him from embezzling more

money, but that didn't quite work either. She'd still lose her style of living in his death, the same as if he was arrested and the police took back the ill-gotten funds. At least if he went to prison, she'd still have been able to continue living in this house, and she'd have Donald's inherited wealth.

"We can't shoot her." Rebecca's hand was still on his forearm. "The neighbors will hear. We'll never be able to get the blood cleaned up before the police get here."

Leon jerked his head in the direction of the back of the house. "Not if we take her into the woods. We'll be far enough away people will think it was a car backfiring or a kid shooting off fireworks."

Rebecca's gaze darted between Leon, the gun, and me. I couldn't tell if she genuinely didn't want him to kill me or if she just didn't want to be caught.

Either way, I needed to feed her fear. "If you leave my body in the woods, they'll still track it back here. Proximity matters."

Rebecca's hands shook. "She's right."

"You could tie me up and leave me here. By the time someone found me, you could be out of the country."

That might be true, and I might be letting potential murderers get away by suggesting it. But the odds seemed good that I could either get out of the ropes, make enough noise that the neighbors would call for help, or be missed before they could actually leave the country. The odds were better than if they shot me anyway.

"Do you think we're stupid?" Leon's grip on the gun tightened.

I flinched instinctively, but he didn't fire.

"We'd have to leave our whole lives behind, and we'd never be able to stop looking over our shoulders."

Rebecca was shaking so hard her ear rings swayed. "It was an accident. We could tell them it was an accident."

She couldn't mean what he planned to do to me. My death wouldn't be an accident.

She'd also used the past tense. She had to mean Donald's death, but you couldn't accidentally give lime juice to someone who knew they shouldn't have it. Especially since he needed a large dose.

My mind was calm the way it sometimes went when I used to think Jarrod was about to kill me and I'd considered which parts of my body to try to protect to prevent my death. The state wouldn't last. It never did once the pain and adrenaline kicked in. Still, for the tiniest moment, it gave me a feeling of control.

"An accident means you'll get manslaughter. You'd be out of prison in a few years. If you kill me, it'll be premeditated murder. You could get life."

I had no idea if any of that were actually true, but it sounded good. All I needed was two more steps to the door and I could reach the handle.

I slid my foot back.

"Stop. Moving." Leon emphasized each word in a sharp staccato. His gaze flickered to Rebecca too quickly for me to take advantage of his gap in attention. He kept the gun trained on me with one hand and laid a hand over her hand with the other. "We'll go far enough into the woods that we can dump her body in the lake. We'll burn our clothes when we get back so there's no chance of evidence turning up on us."

A trickle of panic filtered into my mind. The door wasn't an option anymore, and he had a solid plan now. I didn't have an equally solid plan for getting loose.

"Show her out the back way, Rebecca," Leon said.

Rebecca went first, keeping enough distance between us that I couldn't grab her and use her as a shield. Leon pressed the gun against my spine.

I should probably try to get away anyway, Make as big a mess in this house as possible, so they weren't likely to get away with this.

The problem was that I didn't want to die. As long as I was still breathing, there was a chance I could get out of this. It's what I told myself for years with Jarrod. It's what kept me hanging on to the hope that I'd get away from him some day rather than simply giving up and overdosing on a cocktail of whatever I could put together from the medicine chest.

We went through the kitchen and out through a small door at the back. A sidewalk led around to the front of the house, suggesting this was the servants' entrance. The back of the house butted up to a wooded lot, just as Leon had said. The trees were thick, but the start of a trail was clear. Rebecca headed straight for it. She didn't strike me as the outdoorsy type so perhaps they'd used the trail to meet before.

I had to keep them talking. Maybe I could make Rebecca second-guess this choice.

"You'll still have to get rid of my car. If you get in, all it will take is a single hair for the police to connect you to it."

"I grew up with a guy who breaks down cars for parts and doesn't ask too many questions. He'll handle it."

If Leon knew a man like that, he hadn't grown up wealthy like the Wells. Maybe that was why he was so determined to be with Rebecca. Taking a woman from a man like Donald would have proved he was finally one of them.

Unfortunately for me, that seemed to mean he also knew all the steps they'd need to take to get away with killing me. My only hope was to turn them on each other. Leon was ready to kill me and move on, but Rebecca seemed hesitant. If it hadn't sounded like the contrary was true, I would have thought Leon killed Donald and Rebecca was the unwilling accomplice there too. But it sounded like Rebecca had somehow accidentally killed Donald and Leon knew.

Rebecca was the one who least wanted to kill me now.

The trees grew more densely along the edges of the path. We were probably halfway to the lake, if I remembered my geography correctly. The trees would thin as we got closer.

I had to drive a wedge between Rebecca and Leon. She'd

broken up with him. In hindsight, that was likely out of guilt, but she'd still done it.

"If you go through with this, you'll have to elope. Otherwise, the police can force you to testify against each other."

Rebecca flinched.

"We can do that," Leon said. "It's what we wanted anyway."

"I don't want to get married," Rebecca said softly. "How can I remarry after what I did to Donald?"

Leon's head swiveled toward her. "You didn't mean for that to happen. It shouldn't prevent us from being happy."

We passed a tree, and I ducked behind it and ran.

Leon cursed.

I pumped my legs harder, dodging left and right behind trees to make myself a harder target to hit.

Footsteps sounded behind me but no gun shot. He must be worried that shooting at me could draw too much attention. People might mistake a single gunshot for something else, but if he fired multiple shots, someone was sure to call the police. Once that happened, Leon might still be able to kill me, but he wouldn't be able to dispose of my body. He clearly didn't want to take that risk.

My lungs burned. I hadn't been going running as regularly as I used to. And something that felt a lot like panic clawed at my throat, trying to choke me. I couldn't let it. If I lost control, I'd die here.

I slid behind a tree big enough to cover me from side to side.

Leon gained on me, and I didn't know where I was anymore. I might be headed toward the house or to the lake and right into his plan for all I knew.

If he got a clear shot at me, he'd take it to prevent me from escaping. I had to take a chance and try to knock the gun from his hand.

I picked up a large branch. The bark bit into my palms, and my shoulders ached from holding it, but it was the only one heavy enough to possibly work.

I held my breath, so I could hear Leon's approach over my own ragged gasps.

He paused just before my tree, as if he wasn't sure which direction I'd gone in.

Far back, the snap of twigs and muffled cries of annoyance marked Rebecca closing on our position as well.

Leon took another step forward. His nose and the gun became visible.

I swung the branch. It connected with his wrist, and the gun flew through the air.

The string of curse words he let out would have made a Marine blush.

He tackled me. I lost my hold on the branch and hit the ground. What little air I'd been able to suck in rushed from my lungs. It felt like someone had caved in my chest.

Before I could react, Leon straddled my hips and pinned my

hands to the ground, his grip so tight I could feel the movement of my bones.

Blackness filled the edges of my vision. He was too close. Too close.

It'll be over soon, Fear said. *Stay still and he won't hurt you as much.*

No, that was the wrong advice this time. This time, if I didn't do something, I'd be dead for sure. I fought against his grip, but he was too strong. His grip on my arms, his weight on my waist didn't even move. I couldn't get enough air, and I wasn't sure if it was because he was pressing on my ribs as well or because my brain was shutting down.

"Hurry up, Rebecca." Leon's words were gruff and hard at the edges. "You need to get the gun."

This was what Dan and I had practiced for. I'd spent the last few weeks learning what to do if this happened. I just had to stay calm enough with this man touching me to do what I knew to do. Hold focus for a few minutes, and I might be able to break free. Be brave enough to move close rather than pulling away. I could do this. Dan believed I could, or he wouldn't have spent so much time training me.

I sucked in as much air as I possibly could, and my chest released a little bit. The weight on it wasn't Leon. It was Fear. I knew how to handle him, too, if I could stay focused.

I shifted my head slightly, following Leon's gaze. The gun lay in a pile of leaves not five feet away. Rebecca was a red spot in the woods, but she was coming. I had to get to the gun before either she or Leon did.

Leon's weight was angled forward, pinning my wrists to the ground. I'd get only once chance to catch him off guard and unbalance him. Dan's countermove involved me using my hips to shove him forward. The natural reaction would be for him to let go of my wrists to break his fall rather than landing on his face. I'd then have a split-second to take control from there.

It might work. It might not. But it was my only chance.

I shifted my feet into a position where I had leverage and did exactly what Dan had showed me.

Leon toppled forward and released my wrists.

I swung my arms back, imagining a snow angel and then latched onto his waist as if I were a baby monkey. I looped one of my arms around one of his and threw us into a roll. He went down, and I was on top. I scrambled out of his reach and dove for the gun.

My fingers closed around the gun at the same time as his closed around my ankle.

I twisted enough so that I could point the gun at his face. "Let go."

He did. He shifted back and sat on the moist ground, and I scooted back away from him, until my back pressed against another tree. Rebecca stood at the edge of my vision.

"Sit next to him cross-legged, and then call the number I give you and ask for Detective Dan Holmes. I'll tell you what to say after that."

The adrenaline was draining from my body. Everything trembled. I tightened my grip around the gun and prayed that I wouldn't black out before Dan could reach me. I just had to stay focused.

22

*P*eople were shouting. I heard them, but I couldn't remove my gaze from Leon and Rebecca. If I let my focus drop, they'd hurt me. I had to hold on until Dan got here. He'd bring help.

"Stand down," a familiar voice yelled. "Step away."

Dan's voice. It didn't sound like it was directed at me. I wanted to turn and look at him, make sure it was him, but I couldn't. I couldn't let my attention shift at all or I'd be dead. More than once Leon had tried to move and get closer.

"She took us hostage," Leon said to someone standing behind me. "We need help."

Rebecca nodded. Her mascara had run down her face, but I couldn't remember her crying.

"Quiet," I said. "No talking."

They both clamped their mouths shut. A couple of times

they'd tried to whisper to each other. I'd had to stop them then too because they could have been planning to rush me and take the gun back. I didn't want to die out here in the woods.

"She's a trauma survivor." The familiar voice again. "She's in shock. She's the one who was attacked, and anything she's done was self-defense."

Lots of voices. It sounded like they were arguing.

Someone sat beside me. They smelled familiar, like coffee and soap.

"I need you to give me the gun," he said.

"I can't. They'll kill me."

"They won't." The voice sounded so much like Dan. "As soon as you give me the gun, we can move in and arrest them."

If it was Dan, I could trust him, but I couldn't take my gaze off of Leon and Rebecca to check. If it was Dan, he'd take care of it.

A hand slid over one of mine. The touch was so familiar. My hands ached, my knuckles white. I didn't want to have to watch them anymore. I was so tired.

"Dan?"

"It's me. Give me the gun, okay?"

I nodded and let it fall into his hands. He must have handed it away because the next thing I knew, his arms wrapped around me.

Then I was up in the air, secure against his chest, and we were moving.

"Sir," the man's voice was young and sounded far away. "Shouldn't we take her in to give a statement at least. She was holding two people at gunpoint."

"Would you expect to immediately question a victim who was bleeding out?"

"Of course not, sir."

"We need to show as much compassion for victims' mental health as we do for their physical health. I'll take her statement tomorrow when she's feeling up to it. Right now, I'm getting her checked out by the paramedics and taking her to get some rest."

I must have faded out because the next thing I remembered was a woman in a uniform leaning over me and examining the purplish-blue marks around my wrists. I thought I saw a camera flash.

And then the blackness finally took me.

OPENING MY EYES NEXT FELT A BIT LIKE PEELING WALLPAPER OFF a wall. I stretched my legs and arms slowly. They all worked, but I wasn't going to be running marathons or practicing self-defense moves any time soon. Not unless I was a masochist who enjoyed pain.

The day before came back to me in bits. My heart rate picked up.

I turned my head. I was back in my own bedroom. Dan sat

beside my bed instead of Janie like the last time I'd gotten myself almost killed and needed rest. This time felt worse somehow. Like they'd managed to attack my brain as well as my body.

He hadn't noticed I was awake. His head was bent over a massive book, reading.

Watching him when he didn't know it felt strange. I'd never had the opportunity to do it before. He looked older than when he was in motion, but no less handsome. His cheeks had a dusting of stubble on them that I loved, as if he hadn't wanted to take the time to shave in the past day or two.

My heartbeat slowed back to normal as if it knew we were safe with Dan in the room. More than anything, that felt unnatural. I'd spent so long looking over my own shoulder and watching my own back. To have someone I finally felt I could trust to sometimes take my burden off of me...it must be what an animal who'd been caged felt when they got to run again for the first time.

"What are you reading?" I asked. My voice sounded like I needed a throat lozenge.

Dan didn't jump or start the way I would have. Instead, he set the book aside almost languidly. "The story of Joseph. I read it regularly to remind myself that when bad things happen to good people God is still in control, and he has a plan, even if we don't understand it at the time."

My memory of the story of Joseph in the Bible wasn't as fresh as it probably should be. "Read it to me?"

Dan picked up the Bible like it was the most natural thing in the world for me to ask.

Joseph, it turned out, had been sold into slavery by the brothers he should have been able to trust, was falsely accused of a crime he didn't commit and sent to prison, and was forgotten by the friends he helped. Through it all, he stayed faithful to God, and in the end he was able to do things that helped a lot of people. *What you intended for evil,* he told his brothers at the end of the story, *God intended for good.*

Everything Joseph went through, he went through so that he would end up in a place where he could help people.

Maybe that was why I'd gone through the things I'd gone through too. If I hadn't, I wouldn't have been in Lakeshore when Janie needed rescuing. I wouldn't have been able to help solve the murder investigations I'd found myself embroiled in.

I could see why that story gave Dan comfort. "You should share that with Claire. She once asked me if I knew how you managed to do and see what you do and see every day."

He set the book side again. "I'll do that. How are you feeling?"

I looked down at one of my wrists and rotated it slowly. More stiff than actually painful. "About how you'd expect. How long have I been asleep?"

"Almost a day."

The last time I'd slept that long had probably been when I was a kid with the flu. "Rebecca Wells and Leon Schwab?"

"Looking at a lot of prison time for murder, attempted murder, and accessory after the fact."

That had happened fast. "How did you...?"

I didn't even know how to phrase the question for everything I wanted to know about what had happened after I passed out.

Dan scooted his chair closer but didn't try to touch me. The memory of how he'd carried me in his arms flooded my mind, and heat burned my cheeks. I smoothed down my hair to help hide my face. *Mess* probably didn't begin to describe how I looked right now.

"It wasn't making sense to me," Dan said, "as to why Rebecca and Leon would have pulled a gun on you."

It hadn't made sense to me either at first. "I think Rebecca might have accidentally caused Donald's death somehow."

Dan smiled that smile that crinkled the corners of his eyes and sent a shiver through my heart. "You should have been a detective."

I shrugged against the pillow and propped myself up better. "Baking is safer."

"Is it?"

"It should be."

Dan chuckled. "We got a subpoena for the lawyer's files. The judge deemed it admissible under special circumstances because Kirkland isn't a criminal attorney and his files weren't related to attorney-client privilege of a crime. They were generic paperwork that any lawyer would file."

I didn't fully understand what privilege did and didn't cover. I made a mental note to ask Nicole next time I talked to her. My brain stumbled on the thought. I didn't make a routine of contacting Nicole, in order to protect her from Jarrod.

I peeked at Dan. Not calling Nicole was one of many things I wanted to do but didn't in order to protect myself and others from Jarrod.

"It turned out Rebecca had been asking about powers of attorney and under what circumstances an adult could be deemed incompetent and their care be assigned to someone else."

The final pieces slipped into place in my brain. "She gave Donald lime juice to make him hallucinate, so she could have him ruled incompetent. That's why she said it was an accident. She hadn't meant to kill him. Keeping him alive and still married to her would have given her control over his money in a way that divorce or death wouldn't have.

Dan nodded. "Once I had that information, I played Leon off of her and suggested she was blaming it all on him. He turned on her to save himself. He told us everything she'd confessed to him after the fact, when he was trying to convince her not to break off their relationship."

That explained everything. Almost. "Why did he have a gun?"

The first thing that jumped to my mind was that he'd

planned a murder-suicide for that day if she hadn't changed her mind.

"It was a gift. He planned to give it to her for self-defense because he thought people were still following her around for information on Donald. He thought she'd feel safer if she had some way to protect herself if someone took it to the next level and broke into her house."

Poor man. In a twisted way, he'd truly cared about Rebecca, so much so that he'd been willing to cover up her crimes and even kill for her.

I studied Dan's face again. His dark hair and slightly crooked nose. His bright blue eyes with the laugh lines at the corners.

He was a handsome man, but his heart was even better.

He raised an eyebrow. "What?"

Answering that question felt even riskier than telling him my real name had or telling him about Jarrod had.

But it also felt like he'd earned that honesty and level of trust.

"Thank you. For looking after me." The words caught in my throat, but I forced them out. "For not giving up on me. For believing in me."

He smiled again. "Always. That's what friends do, like I told you."

Friends.

It echoed so many conversations we'd had, but the one that stood out most anymore was the one in Elijah's office when I told him friendship was all I could have with anyone.

The way my heart felt like it was bruising in my chest was my own fault. I hadn't kept a close enough watch on my own emotions.

I could live with the repercussions. I had to if I wanted to keep Dan's friendship. And I did. I'd be willing to hurt every time I looked at him so long as I didn't lose him completely. I'd take every day I could get with him and Janie until he found someone who could give him what he wanted. What he deserved. Then I'd have to accept being relegated to the periphery of their lives, hearing about them through Claire.

Dan got to his feet and pressed a finger to the cover of the Bible. "I'll leave this here in case you want to read the stories of Job and Ester next. They're ones I turn to as well."

I slid the Bible onto the bed next to me. "Thank you."

He nodded. "I'll bring Janie by later if that's okay. I had Claire keep her at my place in case you needed a little time once you woke up to…process things. I'll still need to take your statement today too."

"I can write it out for you. I think it'd be easier that way."

He looked at me as if he wanted to come back and press another kiss to my forehead. He stepped back instead. "I'll bring you a pen and paper."

He turned toward the door, then turned back to face me. His hand went to his pocket.

I let him stand in silence. I didn't know what to say or why he'd turned back.

He pulled a business card from his pocket and handed it to me. The edges were worn, as if he'd been carrying it around and handling it for days.

I glanced down at it. The card was for a divorce lawyer.

"I asked around. He's supposed to be good at cases with unusual circumstances." Dan's voice was low and more hesitant than I'd ever heard from him before. "Life is short, and so much in it is hard. I want us to have a chance at something I think could be good. I'm willing to take the risk if you are."

LETTER FROM THE AUTHOR

I can't believe we're already halfway through the story I planned out for Isabel. I hope you've enjoyed walking alongside her for this new story.

With this book, I wanted Isabel to move another step away from merely surviving. I wanted her to start thinking about what she'd want her life to look like if she were free to chose. Hope is such a valuable, powerful thing. This is the book where Isabel starts to find it.

In the next book, you'll find out what Isabel decides about her relationships and her business. And, of course, there will also be a murder! The next book is called *A Sampling of Murder*.

If you want to know when the next Cupcake Truck mystery releases, make sure to sign up for my newsletter at www.subscribepage.com/cupcakes.

And if you enjoyed this book, I'd really appreciate it if you'd leave an honest review on Amazon or Goodreads. Reviews help fellow readers know if this is a book they might enjoy. Even a short sentence helps!

Love,

Emily

MAPLE SYRUP MYSTERIES

Looking for something to read until the next Cupcake Truck Mystery comes out? Try Emily James' Maple Syrup Mysteries. This thirteen book series is complete and available in both print and ebook formats. The first four books are also available as audiobooks.

Criminal defense attorney Nicole Fitzhenry-Dawes thought that moving to the small Michigan tourist town of Fair Haven and taking over her uncle's maple syrup farm would keep her far away from murderers, liars, and criminals. She couldn't have been more wrong...

If you love small-town settings, quirky characters, and a dollop of romance, then you'll enjoy this amateur sleuth mystery series.

Pick up the whole series at https://smarturl.it/maplesyrupmysteries.

RECIPE: MANGO-COCONUT CUPCAKE

Don't worry — there's no lime in Isabel's tropical cupcakes, so you can eat this even if you're on a cold medicine! These cupcakes do have a lot of steps, but they're well worth the time.

INGREDIENTS:

CAKE

　　1 1/3 cups all-purpose flour

　　1 1/2 teaspoons baking powder

　　1/4 teaspoon salt

　　1/3 cup unsalted butter, melted

　　1 cup granulated sugar

　　1 large egg, at room temperature

　　1/4 cup plain Greek yogurt, at room temperature

　　3/4 cup coconut milk, at room temperature

3/4 teaspoon coconut extract

1/4 teaspoon vanilla extract

1/2 teaspoon almond extract

MANGO CURD

2/3 cup mango pulp (from 1 medium mango)

3 tablespoons granulated sugar

1/2 tablespoon lemon juice

1 1/2 tablespoons cornstarch

pinch of salt

2 large egg yolks

1 1/2 tablespoons cold unsalted butter, cut into small pieces

ICING

1/2 cup unsalted butter, softened

1 1/4 cups powdered sugar

1 teaspoons vanilla extract

1/2 teaspoon coconut extract

TOPPING

2/3 cup sweetened shredded coconut

INSTRUCTIONS:

TO MAKE THE CAKE

1. Preheat oven to 350 degrees F, and line a muffin pan with cupcake liners.

2. In a large bowl, whisk together flour, baking powder, and salt. Set aside. These are your dry ingredients.

3. In a medium bowl, beat together the butter and sugar until light in color and smooth. This will take about 3-4 minutes.

4. Add in the egg, coconut milk, yogurt, vanilla extract, coconut extract, and almond extract and mix until smooth. These are your wet ingredients.

5. Add the dry ingredients to your wet ingredients, and whisk together until combined.

6. Fill the cupcake liners 2/3 full with the batter.

7. Bake for 18 minutes or until a toothpick comes out clean.

TO MAKE THE CURD

1. In a blender or food processors, puree the mango until smooth. You should have 1 cup mango puree at the end. If not, puree a bit more until you get the right amount.

2. In a medium sauce pan, whisk together mango puree, sugar, lemon juice, cornstarch, and salt.

10. In a separate small bowl, whisk the egg yolks, then whisk the yolks into the mango mixture.

3. Whisking constantly, cook over medium heat until the mixture thickens to a pudding consistency. This should take about 5-7 minutes.

4. Remove from the heat and stir in the butter, a few chunks at a time, until dissolved.

5. Use a fine-mesh sieve to strain the mixture. (A rubber spatula works well to push the mixture through the sieve.)

6. Place plastic wrap onto the surface of the curd to stop a skin from forming.

7. Refrigerate for at least 4 hours.

TO MAKE THE ICING

1. Using the whisk attachment for your mixer on medium-high speed, whip the butter for 5 minutes.

2. Reduce the speed to low (unless you like breathing in a powdered sugar cloud). Gradually add the powdered sugar and mix until smooth.

3. Add in the vanilla extract and coconut extract. Beat on medium-high until incorporated.

4. Whip at the same speed for about 2 minutes, until the icing is fluffy.

TO TOAST THE COCONUT

1. Preheat over to 350 degrees F.

2. Place the coconut on a baking sheet lined with parchment paper.

3. Bake coconut until lightly browned. Stir partway through. How long this takes depends on your oven, but the average is 5-10 minutes.

TO ASSEMBLE THE CUPCAKES

1. Cut a hole in the center of the cupcakes, and reserve the piece you cut out.

2. Fill the hole with 1 to 1 1/2 teaspoons of mango curd.

3. Top with icing.

4. Add 1-2 teaspoons of toasted coconut to the top of each.

Makes 12-16 cupcakes.

ABOUT THE AUTHOR

Emily James grew up watching TV shows like *Matlock*, *Monk*, and *Murder She Wrote*. (It's pure coincidence that they all begin with an M.) It was no surprise to anyone when she turned into a mystery writer.

Alongside being a writer, she's also a wife, an animal lover, and a new artist. She likes coffee and painting and drinking coffee while painting. She also enjoys cooking. She tries not to do that while painting because, well, you shouldn't eat paint.

Emily and her husband share their home with a blue Great Dane, six cats (all rescues), and a budgie (who is both the littlest and the loudest).

If you'd like to know as soon as Emily's next mystery releases, please join her newsletter list at www.subscribepage.com/cupcakes.

She also loves hearing from readers.

www.authoremilyjames.com
authoremilyjames@gmail.com

Made in the USA
Middletown, DE
14 July 2023

35136353R00128